THE HIDDEN
KINGME??

DAIRE CYLENCE

WESTBOW
PRESS®
A DIVISION OF THOMAS NELSON
& ZONDERVAN

WestBow Press books may be ordered through booksellers or by contacting:

WestBow Press
A Division of Thomas Nelson & Zondervan
1663 Liberty Drive
Bloomington, IN 47403
www.westbowpress.com
844-714-3454

ISBN: 978-1-6642-2354-7 (sc)
ISBN: 978-1-6642-2353-0 (e)

Print information available on the last page.

WestBow Press rev. date: 05/19/2021

CONTENTS

I want to thank God, THAT IF GOD IS FOR ME THEN WHO CAN BE AGAINST ME!! I thank God for getting me this far for this blessed opportunity to tell my amazing true story through Lighthouse Christian Publishing.

I also love to thank my wife Kim Butter Cylence that through it all has continued to still love me thru it all. God truly gave me a queen who has blessed us with two wonderful children. I thank God for keeping our family strong through the storm of my life, to see my story become a real blessing to others.

I like to thank God that although I had a that father but was still that fatherless. God blessed me to meet a new spiritual father my Pastor, Apostle, Dr. Richards. Who God has put in my life to speak Gods word into my heart of healing and open my eyes to write my testimony. It brought closure to my past life to go forward for my new family to have a Victorious future together with Jesus Christ.

In drafting this true story and my testimony, I hope that people will be able to see the evidence that from a Victim you can be truly Victorious. I hope this book helps other see that nothing is too difficult for the Lord to do, and that it is not over until God says it is over. I also want this book to tell all abused and molested men, women, and children that you can overcome with God. May this book help others see that H.E.L.P (Healing, Encouragement, Living, Past Free) has no age limit. God Bless!!! Daire Cylence

1

A VERY SMALL SURFACE

hough I was born in Philadelphia, I later moved to Camden New Jersey and there my family and me lived in a row house which had a front and back yard. In 1977, I began the third grade, attending school with my two brothers Terance and Jevone, my baby sister Bernadette and baby brother Kevin stayed at home with my mother. My that father worked the second shift at a cake factory, sometimes not coming home until midnight and we rarely saw him, he often surprised us with cake from work.

Later that year; my mother went back to working as a secretary at a nearby office and during that time that father would take care of us as my brothers and I went to school. We still had to share rooms together near the kitchen and my baby brother Kevin, sister Bernadette slept in the room Upstairs near mother and that father. It was difficult taking care of five kids in those days, and even more so when my parents did not get paid. Those weeks without pay were extremely rough that on one occasion I remember waiting for that father to come home with food that all we had to eat were pickles.

Several years passed and I was still attending Elementary School, about to enter the fifth grade, and Terance was 12yrs old entering 6th grade and Jevone 10yrs old entering 4th grade. School was nice although I was still a little nervous shy kid but still having my brothers with me at the same school helped a lot. Our family was always close knit or that's what I thought.

One day, my brothers and I came home from school to find that mother was already at work. That father was about to leave for work so he had asked our Cousin Sidney to watch us. We loved having Sidney around because there was nothing that she couldn't cook and everything she made was delicious too. That day was cold and dreary but my brothers and I begged Sidney to allow us to play outside. So, all 3 of us went outside on our neighboring field and continued to play even as the temperature continued to drop. On the edge of the field was a frozen pond so we decided to have ice races. Terance and I wanted to race on the ice though it was a thing to do but we still did, so we started running and I was about to beat Terance when all the sudden the next thing happened. I slipped and fell and that's all I remember until later I finally woke up with Terance carrying me running to the house with Jevone too crying as I was bleeding from my head. I had tripped and fallen on the ice, cutting my forehead and was dizzy but could hear Jevone yelling for Sidney towards the house. She came outside meeting us at the front door as we sounded far away, then saw me went to get wet towels to pressed against my head, once the bleeding subsided, Sidney put ice on it. My wound wasn't that serious so there was no need to go to the hospital. Sidney still watched me to make sure I did not have a concussion and calmly explained everything to mother when she returned home from work.

Though much of our childhood was filled with simple delights and some happy times my parents sometimes would do some fun nights of enjoy watching movies and music to for the family. However, there was a shadow that continually appeared within our household.

At times when my brothers and me came home and found our parents in an intense argument that one time I heard them arguing and ran up the steps to living room saw our that father yelling at mother. I started crying saying "Stop It Just Stop It!." My parents heard me and mother came over to me toward the couch, saying, "Stop it, stop it!" I then just ran back toward my room when I fell and hit my head on the couch handle and was crying in pain, seeing double vision and began screaming like as my brothers and sister were upset as well. My mother took me into the bathroom and calmed me down apologizing and put a cold rag over my eyes. She told me to keep it over my eyes for a little while and I just listen to her. Still trying to tell myself that my parents loved each other in some type of way hoping things would go back to normal our that father still had to go work late. Sidney would still watch us when she could but then mother and that father started having oldest brother Terance watch us when that father had to leave for work. Often when our mother came home from work, she was exhausted and did not want to be bothered with us. One time we had made a mess of the house and when mother came home, she would let us have it and we just head up to our rooms even when she had a difficult day at work too. But, despite how many times it happened we still loved her dearly.

For a couple of years, we stayed in Camden, then in 1980 our parents decided they wanted to move to Philadelphia, around Southwest. Moving to the "big city" we could only afford a small house and it was quite a transition for us all even me though the school was only couple blocks down the street. We had to cross this big expressway to get to school which was often dangerous. Called "The Sanders School," it was a large building. I was a little nervous so my brothers and I continued to stick together at the new school as that father told us to be brave.

When we went to this school and I was 12yrs old and in 7th grade. We tried to be brave as some of the students were nice but many weren't that they tried to mess with me at times. The month of September seemed to go by quickly that it soon was October and getting a little cold out. I went to school staying quiet and shy that when the last class was over, I ran right outside to meet Terance and Jevone so we can walk home together. We start talking to each other asking how our day was at school as this was our only time to have some kids fun before we get home as our parents were still stressed out since we moved.

2

TEST OF TURMOIL

One day, after coming home from school, we were relaxing playing around in the house when we received a phone call from the factory saying our that father had been hurt on the job. We were all Upset and unsure of the extent of his injury so Terance called mother at work and told her that father was hurt on the job and they took him to hospital. Mother left work early and went to the hospital while we anxiously waited at home for news on our that father. Hours went by before our mother called us saying she was with him and that he had broken his left arm.

They took a few x-rays and found that father had broken bones in his elbows and was advised to stay in the hospital for a while. We then tried to reach out to family members available to drive mother and that father home in our family car when he is discharged. Still my siblings and me waiting at the house hoping he was okay and healing that father was in the hospital for couple of weeks and our mother took off work to be with us kids and help more at home. While we went to school, she stayed home with Bernadette and Kevin keeping the house together. It was hard for us to go to school and concentrate under these circumstances that each day she would tell us not to cry and that he would be home soon. That made all of us feel better but we still missed him a lot as mother had to do everything and it was also difficult that she had to catch the bus every time she went to the hospital to see him.

That week was she did a lot but that Friday mother called us after we came home from school saying our that father would be coming home. We were able to get family drive that father car home with mother in it as he had a brace on both his arms and wasn't able to bend it so he wasn't going back to work any time soon.

When he came thru the door, we were so happy to see him and loved our that father and knew he worked hard to make ends meet for the family. It was Upsetting to see him in such pain and during the first few days he was home we were happy to see him. Our joy was cut short when our mother received a phone call saying the cake factory blamed that father for the accident and would not be paying any extra money while he was out of work.

With his arms hurt he needed to rest and heal so he was limited on any activity even the slightest mobility. I tried to take on the role as leader and calm everybody down but still that father was becoming more Upset with his inability to be the strong figure he once was. In addition, our mother felt increased pressure each day as well especially regarding the only one bringing in money for the family.

November was approaching and Thanksgiving was not far away with mother working constantly and still had to take care of that father at night too. Just when she was about to reach her breaking point, we received some good news. The cake factory was still going to pay him a paycheck every two weeks as the investigation of what happened was complete. This was such a blessing for our family.

However, I began to see changes in mother that she was becoming less patient and would start yelling if the house was a mess or dishes had been left in the sink. The stress she endured of having to make dinner, take care of that father and two babies was getting to her. That father would often hit us if we didn't listen to her, still he tried helping her but he couldn't stand long enough to do anything. This continued through November making Thanksgiving an unhappy time Then December came and went without much hope for a Christmas celebration either.

Then something happened that none of us expected. Mother became unhappy with the house, saying it was too expensive and that we couldn't afford it. We wondered *why now and where are we going to move?* That made that father so Upset that he was yelling repeatedly, "We can't move we only been here five months!" Mother still wanted to leave and we were told that we would be moving before December 31st.

Me, Terance, and Jevone went to a new school as I was so scared and didn't talk much, staying to myself. As the weeks went, I was doing okay with unfamiliar environment. Every day, when I got home from school, the family would be packing up things; at times this went all through the night. It was becoming an everyday occurrence from scrubbing the walls to putting everything we didn't wear into trash bags. Before we knew it there was only one week left before Christmas and I didn't see any shopping going on. I guessed mother and that father were using our Christmas money to get a moving van for our new home.

Coming home one day on a Wednesday in December, that father was in his room lying in bed. I asked him if he was okay and he said he needed his pain pills. I gave them to him with something to drink. I asked how we going to move all our stuff to the other house. He said that guess he would be driving because mom can't and we didn't know anyone else who could. He then told me to close the door and take care of Bernadette and Kevin. I just walked away thinking that idea was completely .

Days passed by and the weekend arrived with things not going any better because we were still cleaning and packing up, moving furniture toward the door so it be easier to get everything into the truck. My brothers and me were doing most of the work and mother helped as best as she could.

Soon it was the week of Christmas and we didn't have a tree up, which wasn't a surprising. Toward the end of that week that father was telling us we would be moving on December 24th so we could be in the new house by the end of the weekend. I was focused on packing up my things when I came home that Thursday from school. On December 23rd, with two days left before moving, that father had us putting things in the garage that we didn't get to bed until midnight.

That Friday, we went to school barely awake but still made it through the rest of the day. I didn't want to get detention as I was leaving school early walking with Jevone and Terance. They told me they didn't want to move either and didn't understand why we were in the first place. One thing was for sure, if we asked why we would be yelled at or even hit, so we kept our mouths shut.

When we got home, that father was watching Bernadette and Kevin. He told us that we had to have everything moved into the truck so we could take it over to the new place that evening. We started to move items and later when mother came home, that father could then drive our things over there. Mother was tired when she came home from work but she knew we were going to be moving all through the evening and night. We were packing and packing waiting on that father to come back with the moving van repeatedly. Moving furniture from each bedroom; taking the beds apart, then moved the dressers, bringing them down the steps as close as we could toward the garage and the front door.

Later in the evening, when that father came back with the van, we began to move our belongings into the truck, however, that fathers' arms were hurting him badly from lifting. He was walking slowly soon had to sit down, watching as Jevone, Terance and me got into the truck. Later, we were heading to the new house and were extremely tired as it was after nine at night. While we continued to load the truck, we knew it would take a couple of trips before we would be finished as we continued until almost 1am in the morning. All of us were dead tired, but had successfully moved everything into the new house. It wasn't a neat job but it was the best we could do under the circumstances.

That night we went to bed laying on the floor with no beds. We were all thinking about tomorrow and how it would be Christmas day. With all the work we were doing we forgot about it, yet we still hoped we would receive some type of surprise.

When I woke up the next day it was noon, that's how tired me and my brothers were. We didn't pay attention to the fact it was Saturday or even Christmas day. We were able to check out the house and found that it was a little bigger but had no backyard to play in. Mother and that father said the house was our Christmas present though they did buy small toys for each of us.

When my brothers woke up, we ate cereal for breakfast and then continued putting all the furniture where mother wanted it, including the beds for each room. It took the whole weekend to finish and there was no time to enjoy our toys or to relax. Time was going by as we continued to fix up each room, taking the dresser Upstairs too as it was getting later toward afternoon.

We heard kids playing outside but we weren't about to go outside. Later, after we finally got some time to rest, mom and dad came back later in the evening bringing us some food for dinner to eat. All I knew, was that moving into the new house was going to bring the same old problems just at a different address.

3

NO LEGS TO STAND ON

unday was all about cleaning and moving items around. Then we had to get ready to go back to school on Monday, which meant going to bed earlier than before. This was because we had to get up earlier due to the walk being longer to Saint Middle School. Although he couldn't driver mother to work, she asked that father to walk with her to the trolley as we walked to school. The new school was a hard adjustment for me as the kids seemed loud and bold. My brothers on the other hand were adjusting already but I was having an extremely nervous tough time getting thru the first day of school. Eventually I made it through that day and waited for my brothers to walk home with me. We talked about the nice house we had in Camden and having to leave it for the new one. The new school was okay were we had no choice but to adjust.

When we got home, our that father was waiting for us at the door and wanted us to help him with Bernadette and Kevin. He was also angry saying that one of us needed to go to store to pick up some groceries. He was still not feeling well enough to drive, so Kevin and I walked to the store. With this new chore that father gave us, we had to hurry up back home so we could complete our homework. I barely saw my mother once she got home because she was mad and tired from work so I quickly went Upstairs trying not to get yelled at or hit.

With today Thursday, last day of school before the new year, I woke up and just wanted to get this day over with and start the New Year off better.

That father returned home from taking mother to work and we headed to school and that was our last day of school in 1980 with a good day and nobody was mad or upset. We just couldn't wait to get out of there and go home, as I did well through all my classes with no problems and no issues with any of the kids. I didn't feel nervous that day at all and as my classmates were cracking jokes that laughing with them felt great.

My last class was art a happy class as that I ran out of the classroom and waited for my brothers so we could get out of there out there and head home. We didn't want to get caught up in anything silly that Terance, Jevone, and me ran like from school. Looking to have a long weekend hoping it be a peaceful with our family that when I got home saw that father was still in a lot of pain, He asked me to go meet mother at the trolley stop and I just agreed.

When I got to the trolley, there was mother getting off and I went to meet her saying "Hi, mom," telling her that father was in a lot of pain but she didn't want to hear it still upset saying she tired and had a distressing day.

"He should have taken more pills for his back so he could pick me up!" she grumbled. I just kept quiet, only talking about the fact that it was New Year's Eve. I could see she was not listening but I did what I could to calm her down, hoping she wouldn't start yelling and make matters worse.

Heading home, I carried her bags and when we got to the front door of the house when she started yelling at that father for not meeting her at the trolley. He was in the bedroom while Bernadette and Kevin were downstairs with Jevone watching TV and Terance in his room.

She went upstairs and then it started - they were yelling and all I heard was that father saying he was in a lot of pain, but mother didn't want to hear it. All she thought about was that she was not supposed to be walking that far and that he should always be there to pick her up. This continued for hours while we tried to take care rest of house until finally, they stopped and our mother came downstairs to fix dinner like nothing happened.

It was finally quiet while in my room with Jevone and Terance laying down mother was downstairs with Kevin and Bernadette as that father was still trying to sleep. Just after 9:30pm, not long before the New Year, I fell asleep for a little while nobody was fighting and I slept well. That was until Jevone woke me up saying it was January 1, 1981 got up tired but didn't want to miss the event so went downstairs as that father was on the couch with everybody else was watching TV as Mr. Mikel Show was counting down. We had some soda while our parents had wine, then the countdown continued, "5, 4, 3, 2,1 Happy New Year 1981!". I was hoping the New Year would bring peace to the family, with no more fighting that our family act nice to one another, loves each other, otherwise there wasn't much point to celebrate.

On Monday, we woke up to the new year had to run most of the way to school and being athletic, it wasn't a problem for us got there just before the bell rang, sweating like even though it was still cold out, still adjusting to the new school the best we could. I was still a little scared not seeing my brothers or running into them in the halls that I wanted each class to be over quick. As I managed to make it thru to my last class, time for me to escape out going home was getting better too for me with my brothers that it was less fighting between our parents where they talked and got along great!

On the weekends we started to go outside and not let the wintry weather keep us played catch football with our new neighbors joined in as well. Between helping the family and finding time to play, that's about all we did with our time off.

By the end of Spring, I thanked God for helping me make it thru and had just barely pass all my classes to graduate. With Jevone and Terance did well enough as well to move to the next grade, enjoy the summer, and appreciate the new house we were living in!!

This summer we tried to spend as much time outside not to get on our parent's nerves that thank goodness it worked. Heading toward another new school year, I was turning 14 years old in July and would be going to the 8th grade.

Now when you're having such a fun time you try to block out the tough times and that is what I did that sometimes I asked God to help me and my family to make it thru the year. And before I knew it, me and my family had made it through to 1982, a full year and half without problems. I remember 1982 NBA season and The Roadsters were in the playoffs that father bought us shirts to commemorate the event.

It was nice to watch basketball sports with my brothers was one pleasant thing to enjoy. As time was getting better, I knew something would find a way to interfere with some happy times and it did. Later that month our parents told us we had to move again coming with excuses that the house was too small and a single home would be better. It was just a matter of time before we were disappointed again that thinking a normal family life was not going to last long for us. Our faces just dropped as we now understood we couldn't even afford to stay in a home to enjoy.

My brothers and I had just gotten used to being at the new house but time to now move again as later that month we ended up doing that sneaky moving in the middle of the night just as we had done in the past houses. It was another address and a bigger house but more problems to deal with difficult for us to constantly adjust.

On Monday, mother had to get to work and that father found a way to take her driving her to the bus stop in a new location we had no idea how to get registered for school.

Our first week in the new house was okay as that father was sleeping in his room and we were watching TV. We weren't ready to go outside as we didn't feel like meeting the new kids in the neighborhood, instead we just relaxed with each other. We would watch Kevin and Bernadette as that father was sleeping from taking his medicine and my brothers and I would play in the house almost getting on each other's nerves. At times we would be arguing and it would wake up that father coming out yelling at us to stop making noise scared with that father big hands some big heavy hands that we tried to go hiding in separate corners of the house.

With only one week before school, we still didn't know where it was that all we were told is that we would be attending Willows High School address was so far, he took us there that day to register.

The next day, we had to leave at 7 AM to be at school by 7:45 AM. We had to go through a long walkway through a field, finally getting there so we could report to the office. As I went to my class sweating like still worried but seeing my classmates were culturally mixed made me feel a lot better. Still, I was quiet and remained that way through the rest of my classes.

I did notice some pretty girls, but looked away before they could see me staring making myself look weird if they caught me too.

Going from one class to another was a little better but not seeing my brothers Terance or Jevone, still eventually made it thru this first week of school. Later me and my brothers met up outside when school was over and went home together.

When we got home, I could see frustration on that fathers' face because the family car broke down again so he couldn't pick mother up. When she got home, things were bad as she was frustrated having to catch the bus home every day. Each day when she got home, we hear it, they were arguing increasingly. It was costing too much more money for a cab to take mother to the bus stop. So, my brothers and me decided to take turns meeting mother but she was still very unhappy. To get out of that negative atmosphere, me, Jevone, and Terance would go to the store for our parents. However, it started getting dark early and there were no streetlights or corner stores only the one near our school. By the time we got to the store, it was late so we would walk fast to get home.

All I know is somehow God got us through those first few weeks and I did okay in school but was still nervous. My brothers did okay as well but they never said much about the new school.

Then it happened when we came home from schoo hearing our

parents arguing about paying the mortgage. That father thought that by getting this house it would keep mother happy, but he was wrong. His checks were now coming every other week so we were depending on mother's check.

Sometimes on the weekend, me and my brothers would go outside in the backyard and play football after we finished our homework just to get away from our parents arguing. We would have so much fun that we tried to stay outside even longer so our parents wouldn't ruin our joy of a little freedom. At times they would be yelling "get in here!" it was so loud that all the other neighbors could hear it and embarrassing, so we had to go back into that house and endure the storm. Just went to our rooms and hid as best we could.

Since money was tight it was hard to ask for school supplies that often we had to divide the supplies among each other, still luckily, we had our own book bags. Anything else we needed would have to wait a long time that often get looked at funny in school because often had to go through the same clothes over and over, often sharing with my brothers. This made it hard to avoid classmates picking on me and my outfit or sneakers.

Things didn't change much in the new house and in fact they just became more difficult. We tried our best to handle things on our own, like adults, but there was little help.

On the weekend, there was nothing to do but go outside because we were Upset and miserable living in the new neighborhood that one day, we decided to take a chance and go outside to the park. Not as scared with no fear went to play basketball for a while had fun out there until it was evening. When we came home, our parents were angry, saying we were out too long and lucky we had something to eat threats. My brothers and me complained that nothing needed to be done or that no one needed anything from the store. We were learning that it was their way of taking the joy out of everything that still coming in and getting yelled at for no reason but the only positive thing about the new house was that it was big enough to give us unfamiliar places to hide.

4

TWIST OF THE STORM

Though attending Willows High School was now a more positive experience, at home our parents continued to argue that seemed to be steadily increase and this time it was about buying a car. Fall was here and the weather would be getting cooler. With that father tired of our mothers' complaints regarding walking to work, that father decided he would have to do give in which would put us in a tighter financial situation of trying to get a new car. Whatever they had planned to do this always put us in a tough situation where rest of the bills don't get paid and it taken out on us kids.

Going into October was better than the previous month. School was fun but I hated going home that I felt something inside me build up resented my parents because of what they were putting my brothers and sister through. Even Terance and Jevone started acting out in anger because of the cussing and talking to us like we were nothing - calling us unusual and silly that happened to us daily.

One day, that father starting yelling at mother about her not respecting him because he still couldn't drive her to work and around. He also said she didn't appreciate the new house he gave her. This went on for hours until he finally went into his room, slamming doors. We ended up hiding from them, fearing they would take it out on us that we ran outside for the safest place to escape being hit.

The arguing continued daily that we started to see weeks go by and would run out of food, because most of the money was going toward the rent and other bills. At times we would eat the same things repeatedly such as peanut butter and jelly sandwich for lunch and then for dinner too or cereal.

One day after we got home from school, that father let us in, but then told us to just go take care of Kevin and Bernadette and that he needed to lay down. Later we watched a little TV when it was Terances turn to go meet mother and walk her home and I was so happy it wasn't my turn.

It still didn't change the consistent bad weekends that my brothers, sister, and me kept being woke up to more arguing. Our parents were at it in the living room, getting louder and louder and calling each other names. Soon they were in each other's faces, screaming at the top of their lungs then follow each other yelling and slamming doors.

In the kitchen, that father said he had enough of the arguing, feeling he was not being appreciated for the new house and the sacrifices he was making. As they continued yelling, my brothers and I tried to tell them to stop as Bernadette was crying and was upset. Nothing we said mattered because they would forget who was around them including our neighbors. I tried to tell them to stop but was told to shut up with that father in mothers face while she taunted him saying, "You want to hit me, then go ahead!" We just couldn't stop them from arguing and we knew the people in the neighborhood could hear everything. I wanted to call the police but was scared they might take our parents away.

Soon mother was getting angrier with that father and he was yelling at her back as we tried telling them to stop; and were so scared that it seemed like the house was falling apart with all of us crying and our parents kept calling each other bad names using words we never thought they would say in front of Bernadette and Kevin.

Things just worsened with our parents slamming doors at each other as we tried to tell them please stop it but couldn't. It then came to a breaking point when that father just ran out the house again. Terance had had enough and decided to do something about it as he ran right at our that father and said "please, please don't leave us that father" which only turned his anger to just stand there towards Terance. Mother told him to don't leave either as Terance then ran away crying from that father as mother was still crying and upset.

Jevone and I started looking for Terance but as the hours went, we couldn't find him. We went back home and could hear that father in his room trying to calm down. We didn't know what to do still tired from looking for Terance and it was getting late that we really worried and wondered if he was safe.

Later that night Terance finally walked through the door as we Jevone and me ran to hug him. Mother was of course glad to see him too but asked him "Why did you run out of the house?." He explained that he was tired of the arguing and was afraid of that father leaving us for good. Hearing that Terance was back in the house, our that father came out of his room as we were trying to block him from coming at Terance but, he was still glad to see that Terance made it home safely. It was if Terance didn't know that father was going to react but he did hug him. Mother took Terance to his room while that father calmed down and went to sleep in the living room.

We all finally got to sleep that night, but given how Upset everyone in the family was, it was a miracle to get Bernadette and Kevin to stop crying too as they both went to sleep as well with mother.

The following weekend was ruined as we just stayed in our rooms trying to keep away from mother and that father. With the weekend passing we had to get it together Monday for school as it was now toward the end of October we were headed back to school trying to focus on our classes, but with what happened in the house it was difficult. I acted like nothing was wrong the best I could around other kids. But later that week, Terance decided to apologize to that father saying he was sorry about running away with that father standing there with me and Jevone said" okay" and then he walked away. I wasn't sure if he accepted it but we were hoping he would.

It took me a while before I finally had the courage to ask that father about girls and what a boy like me needed to know. I went to his room while he was laying down and asked what I needed to know about girls and about my body. He said "why ask me about that?" I told him that I had started looking at girls a lot more and was getting this feeling when I did. Then said I wanted to know more about sexuality and that father said say okay, but first he talked to me about my body, so he started to tell me that I had to take care of myself.

I started feeling a little better about that father, like he cared, and that he wasn't a bad or useless that father like mother said as he started to talk more, I could see a look of happiness on his face. He was proud of being able to tell his son about this subject saying that boy's bodies are made different than girls. As we talked for a while, my brothers heard what that father was talking about and came into the room to be curious. They started listening more intently and it was time for sons and their that father to come together. I was happy because we still needed our that father whether we liked him or not he was still our that father. He started talking to us also about how he met mother when he was just a boy and she was a young girl. It was funny and interesting to hear how they were married and it made him smile. We continued to listen and then he told us that girls are picky and you can't approach a girl and not know how to talk to them otherwise you will be laughed at. Just talking to him made our time with him better that later during the school week, my brothers and me would talk to him every day. He then began to discuss our hygiene and noticed we had dirty draws and that it was nasty to be having that, especially around girls. I was having a slight problem with my bowls and having little accidents with my sensitive stomach. That father was telling me that I need to take better care of my stuff or I would have problems with the girls. He said that our interest in girls and these conversations were opening the door to a new period in our lives and there was no turning back.

5

THE ENTRY THAT NEVER EXITS

That father said he was going to teach us about the birds and bees and how God made us to like girls. God made parts of our bodies differently from girls and we were supposed to be together as partners. He talked more about when he was young and how he liked girls. He got to know mother as they went to the same school and lived near each other. As we listened, we were happy to be talking with that father as he was in a happy peaceful mood while mother was taking care of Kevin and Bernadette.

During the weekend he told us that when we do find that right girl, we would fall in love and we would want to spend rest of our lives with that girl. "Now you first have to know you have feelings for her and she has them for you," that father said. When you see the girl, it will hit you like a tingling feeling inside while you are starring at a her or find yourself smiling every time you see her.

As it was getting later into the afternoon, mother wanted us to go eat lunch as that father said he would talk to us more later. It was an exciting time in our house; that father and sons talking in a civil voice and it was exactly what we all needed.

Later that evening he got us together talking again saying "You will do some unusual things that will make a girl think you are and that is not an effective way to get a girl to like you, so the best thing you can do is just walk by her and say hi or ask her what her name is." Then that father said it now it was time to talk about our bodies.

During the weekend, that father said he wanted to speak with each of us one on one about our hygiene. He said he wanted to talk to me first, then Jevone and last Terance. He wanted to let us know that we can't have stinky draws and our bodies can't smell either like underarms and wanted to make sure we were taking care of our teeth. I didn't know if he was just talking to me as I did have problems with my stomach and going to the bathroom a lot. That's when he finally said it to me that you can't be messing up your clothes as I put my head down and was about to cry because he said "That is nasty to do at 14 years old -you're too big to be having that happen and nobody will like you if you can't get it together! You will be picked on all the time by kids!" as he was telling me I should take care of myself better. He also told my brothers too, so we would look like clean boys to girls and told us about talking to girls. Talk to them nicely and don't be cussing like the kids do outside in the street. It seemed like a funny thing to say given how our parents would often speak to each other we still talk until it was getting late, we had dinner then had to get ready for school the next day.

On Monday I went to school feeling a little better about myself but still needed to stop messing up my clothes and draws. Walking home from school with my brothers, they saw girls that they liked but were too afraid to say anything.

Once we were home, that father wanted to talk to me more about the birds and bees in our room. He asked me if I liked anybody in my class and I said no. He said okay but started to tell me If I did like a girl my body would become excited but I didn't know what he meant by that so he just said it can get excited. He also explained that we have something inside our body that can make a girl have a family like our mother did and that was our first, real conversation about having a girlfriend. He then said he wanted to show me what he was talking and told me to take my draws off. This made me nervous and I was worried that I might have messed up my draws.

I knew I still had that stomach problem and he told me to stay in my room for a while because he had to take care of Kevin and Bernadette. I was afraid of what he was going to do to me with me having this problem since I was 12 years old. My parents would yell at me all the time because of it, that when that father came back later, he saw my dirty draws mad saying he told me not to do this again and had to do something about this. Knowing I was in trouble he told me that I was being punished for it as I started crying like, but then instead told me to stand in the corner of my room. Still crying, wondering what he was going to do to me, but then something happened I never expected. He came behind me and touched me in a way that really scared me, touching me in a very odd manner. I asked that father what he was doing but he just said be quiet or he would punish me. So, I just stood there, not understanding what was going on crying.

Standing there for those minutes was like hours as scared and confused, said okay can I go now, then that father said "Don't mess up your clothes again or you will get this punishment again!! As I was putting my clothes back on and was still crying and scared as I ran out the room while he was yelling at my brothers saying they were next. I was so scared and in shock that for the rest of the day crying and did this well into the night that wasn't even able to speak to my brothers of what happened to them. All I could do is try to make it thru the night to somehow get it together to go to school next day still in shock.

The situation with my that father had me with such fear that I put toilet paper in my draws to not mess them up. I was going to the bathroom every time. I didn't want to see that father again in that same state of anger and lost my appetite.

Since I was unable to concentrate on my schoolwork properly, my grades were poor on a test in history class, it was a D. When my that father found out he became angry and sent me to my room. I stayed there and thought about what have I done now. So scared waiting and waiting, sweat dripped down my face because I was nervous what that father would do to me. Finally, he came into the room, closing the door and said, "What is wrong with you? Why did you mess up on that test?" I had no answer to give him except sorry, he then told me to drop my pants but thinking he would just give me the belt and that's it. He came behind me hitting me once then twice and was checking my draws seeing they were messed up again. I said it was only a little bit but he was still angry, asking why can't you keep them clean as he hit me again saying just take them off and to stand there.

Next thing I know he was behind me touching me wrong way again inappropriately, then molesting my body. He was telling me it was okay and "I love you, but your mother doesn't love me anymore." He wanted someone to show him love and care while I was still crying and couldn't move. Saying he didn't want to look for love on the street and if I would allow him to touch me inappropriately, he would not leave the family. But also teach me how to take better care of my body and how to deal with girls and that it would make him feel better. Still stunned and scared he leave us just said okay and sorry as he inappropriately touched me again, then left the room.

For this to happen to me again just didn't know what to think. At this point the belt was a better way of teaching me a lesson but wanted to tell mother and my siblings but the thought of that father leaving I had no clue what to do. Feeling ashamed, but come out of my room unable to speak. Just told my brothers that I messed up they were so scared not to get into any trouble that they did their homework immediately. Later Jevone went to meet mother and walk her home as she came in, that father told her what I did wrong and she just came in hollering at me saying I can't mess up in school. She told me that I needed to get it together as I just went right to bed. But couldn't sleep too afraid, hoping not to have bad dreams about what happened.

That last day of school I barely had any sleep was so scared to close my eyes, then waking up late for school, got dressed as fast as

I could and started running to catch up with my brothers. They had left early not wanting to get the belt either after what I had gone through.

When the weekend came, all I did was stay in my room, away from everybody. That father was too embarrassed to even look at me, knowing how he touched me wrong way. My brothers were allowed to go outside, but I couldn't because I was on punishment for my draws. When that father came into my room asking me was I okay, I just said yes, he then said he loved me and was sorry but with what excuse for why he attacked me don't know. I couldn't look at him as my that father to me with him closing the door behind him, just curled up in the bed wanting to be left alone. Mother didn't even checkup on me as usual.

When the weekend ended, I tried to look forward to Monday as it was Halloween week but not in any mood to celebrate as we went back to school. Did what I had to do in each class, getting all my work done, and then heading home slowly. When my brothers and me came home from school that father got a phone call about Jevone getting in trouble in school. So, that father told me and Terance to get out of the room and he let Jevone have it sending him to his room. He later got hit with the belt plenty of times and was crying like, while I just kept quiet and did my homework as Terance did too.

I went to check on Jevone, asking what he did wrong. He was crying and said he got in argument with a classmate and the teacher gave him detention and that father was angry told him he was punished. It was now becoming bad for everyone with me wondering if that father was doing the same thing to Jevone that he was doing to me.

Our brother Terance had a smart mouth and it often got him into trouble as that father was teaching us not to be sloppy and dirty around girls while we were at school. That father often gave Terance the belt and he would try and fight back. Sometimes, trying to avoid that father Terance would run around the room trying to get away, but that made the situation far worse.

After those beatings, he would just stay in his room quiet, wanting to be left alone as Jevone and me didn't bother him. Terance would keep talking loud saying how he was sick of this place and was ready to leave at once. I asked him where he was going to go live at because we didn't have anyone to help us but he said when he graduate 12th grade, he was out of here.

Then later that week we came home from school one day, that father was waiting for us and he said he wanted to talk to me about something. He told Terance and Jevone to take care of Kevin and for somebody to go and get Bernadette from 2nd grade school. He came to me in my room asking if I had done a decent job in school that day. I just said yes, then said that he wanted to check my draws, but I said no telling him I was telling the truth, but he just kept pulling my pants down telling me to turn around.

The next thing I knew he began to touch me inappropriately and I told to him to stop it. "Can I just pull my pants up please!" I yelled. He finally stopped as I pulled my pants up. He said that I better not mess my draws up or else. Angry again had made a fist ready to hit him but it would make things worse with my brothers and I didn't want them to go off on that father too. Being abused by my own that father saddened me that I still was trying to take this abuse for him not to leave us isn't fair to me.

6

COMING OF
YOUR FATE

As Halloween arrived, I remember we didn't even want to go outside because we were Upset from all the abuse. At school, the kids would look at me funny, but it was safer being at school then at home, as I would often see my brothers in the hallway and we would check to see if each other was okay.

The following month of November, it was getting cold out, Terance and I argued a lot with that father as Terance and Jevone were fighting each other at times too. With so much anger in the house, it was getting hard to deal with it, all the fighting and then having to deal with a that father that wanted to touch me inappropriately because he isn't getting love or attention from out mother.

Somehow, I still got through that first week of November in one piece by starting to increasingly praying in my bedroom, asking God to help my family, especially my that father because of how he acted toward me. I asked Him to stop all the dreadful things that were going on in this house.

In school, I was struggling in my English class and the teacher warned me to do better. With the parent's meetings coming up soon, knowing it is time to improve or I'd have to deal with that father touching me. Having two weeks to improve and was doing all my homework, studying, and prepared myself for the quiz.

I was feeling good about my test scores when Wednesday night arrived and my that father came with me for the conference because mother was tired from work. All the teachers were positive except for my history teacher. She said I wasn't doing well at all and that I needed to do better because my average was a D. Going home that night was not good at all, that father kept asking me what the problem was. I was trying to tell him I was doing my best except with you messing with me at home just Upset me and I couldn't concentrate in school all the time with having problems keeping my draws clean.

When we got home, he sent me to my room telling mother what happened. My brothers were asking me what was wrong knowing I was in trouble, real scared telling them I had a D in history and they just got more worried for me.

Later, that father came into the room telling my brothers to get out, then told me to take my pants down and I knew it was going to happen. He asked me what I wanted him to do and I said, "Just please give me the belt!."

When he said turn around all I could do was cry as he hit me three times and then began to touch me inappropriately from behind saying "don't do this again or you will make me angry like never before!." I was praying God please hear my cry!!!

Days went by so nervous going back to school and home, not talking to anybody just wanted to be left alone. My brothers were doing well in their classes to, but when I would go home from school Terance and Jevone told me they were beaten as well but not like me. We were so scared to even go into our own house that if I got out of school sooner, I still be waiting for them be my brothers and me wanted to go into the house together.

Going inside the house, that father told us that we needed to take care of Kevin and Bernadette when we got home from school. He said his back was bothering him and he was in lot of pain yelling at us so we just did what he said and later I had to do my homework and study.

While that father was washing clothes, and waiting for the next load, he came to my room and pulled me to the side saying he found my draws and they still were very dirty. He said I needed to stop messing up my draws because if mother found out she would have a fit, and I would be punished again. He said he was looking out for me and not to forget this as I feared he use this against me to keep touching me inappropriately more!!!.

It was a rough couple of weeks, especially when it became cold out. We had to wear the same clothes from last year, nothing new. Still worrying about that father bothering me I did more like washing my clothes out myself in the bathroom sink or the tub just so that father didn't have a reason to touch me.

Later that night, mother was home and wanted to check on me so just told her I'm okay, doing my homework. She then went downstairs to go cook dinner as that father came in closing the door while my brothers and sister downstairs eating dinner. He told me he found my draws drying in the room and was Upset that I was trying to hide it from him and I got Upset, telling him to leave me alone. He grabbed me by the arm saying, "I'm tired of you doing this!" He then started to pull my pants down, but I told him to stop it and told him that mother and everybody was home. He didn't care as he tried to touch me inappropriately, telling me "I know you have dirty ones on!" I started fighting back for the first time as he grabbed me in a inappropriate way, telling me that he owned it. I yelled at him to get off me or I would tell mother as Terance and Jevone heard me yelling knocking said what's going on and he just left me there crying. With two months to go in 1982, I had to keep it together and started to talk to God more, asking him to help me and to keep me from my that father's touching me and my family safe. It was still hard for my brothers as Kevin and Bernadette didn't know what was going but would cry when our parents argued. My parents didn't seem to realize that it was affecting them and plus Thanksgiving three weeks away, it was difficult to know what we would be thankful for.

I tried my best in school and my grades were getting better with me studying more coming straight home each day, closing, and locking the door to my room, not playing outside. That father was leaving me alone for a while little bit. Mother was still working a lot as the big house was costing us more than they thought it would. Sometimes we barely had food to eat, we were often skipping meals to eat. Mother started to complain saying that we were behind on the bills, yelling at that father to a point they were really going at it for a while; we all just went into our rooms staying away from them as much as possible. Then mother was complaining about walking too much that turned into another argument of our parents decided that to buy another cheap car. That father looked through the papers over the weekend trying to find one. One Sunday, it seemed like a prayer miracle as our parents were in a rarely good mood and let us play outside. We took off like a rocket Terance, Jevone, and me, running out to play basketball before they changed their minds. It was the first time in a long while that we got to have some fun and enjoy being outside.

Being out there for couple hours, we had a wonderful time, but soon it was time to go back home. We walked back to the house laughing about how much fun we had. Jevone and me had played the game Rough House with Terance always winning, but still it was enjoyable being happy for the first time. We walked back into the house and that father told us to go wash up while I just stayed rest of the day in my room where it was safe. It was the best way to end the weekend than I could have ever imagined because that father wasn't bothering me! That night I realized that God had heard my prayer; my prayer to have a safe house and was so thankful he did answer my prayer.

The next day we went to school and that week turned out to be happier than expected feeling better I started talking a little to my classmates and even had enough courage to speak to this one girl name Stacy that I thought was nice. She would often say hi to me, but I would just mumble back and would stare at her because she was cute.

It was really turning out to be a fun week. Later, I walked with my brothers back home. It was still cold, but we still had fun and we hoped our happy attitude would rub off on our parents. Everything at home went well and that father even had dinner ready for us. They were in a good mood and we could hear that father talking about how he found a car for us to buy. I was happy to hear that as we needed one.

The following week was another good one. Our parents were getting ready to go get the new car from a dealership in New Jersey. We stayed home and I was enjoying having fun with Bernadette and Kevin[1] was watching cartoons on TV with Jevone and Terance chilling in room as this continued until later, they finally came back. From what I saw it was that father pulling up with a new car for us. It was two toned red and tan, nice and clean too. I ran outside the house see it didn't care it was cold out, Terance, Jevone and Bernadette were happy to see mother in the passenger side just as happy and we went inside glad to see the new transportation. Just seeing that car outside of the house was a wonderful thing to see.

Going back to school I wanted to tell somebody how much of a fun time I had with my family and that we had a new car. I still didn't have any friends to talk to and was in my shy mode for a while but it was okay because just seeing those couple weeks that went by with a calm house what a relief.

The following week was Thanksgiving and was looking forward to us at least celebrating one good evening together. However, later that father told us we were moving Wednesday, the night before Thanksgiving. Another running away from bills move. I was upset that my grades were suffering because of this.

Out last week in that house I was walking home from school that Wednesday morning with my brothers saying we going to miss this place and we didn't even get a chance to meet new friends. After 10 pm that father got the Handler truck. It took us a couple hours back and forth until finally we ended up moving back to the old house on Mercury Place in Philadelphia. We got everything into the house then went to sleep dead tired and was woken up next day to Thanksgiving Day. All we did was clean and move stuff back into our old rooms; I stayed in room with my brothers trying to sleep through the weekend but still didn't know when we were going back to school. Monday morning, we had to register for school once again.

We woke up almost late on the first day of school and I was nervous but kept it together as we walked together. My classmates didn't bother me yet but I was almost shaking even up until my last class. I ran out that classroom to outside of the school to wait for my brothers. We got home that father was there asking how our day was. I just said it was okay in a faint voice and my brothers said the same. Then immediately went to my room check my draws to make sure I didn't have an accident, had a small one on cleaned up. Finally, the weekend came and December arrived while my brothers and I were in the house watching cartoons.

It was my happiest moment and enjoyed it while if I could since it was a short week with us having early dismissal that's when my brothers and I were playing all the way home. Later, that father went to get mother so it was a nice night safer to be outside my room and playing in the house. We relaxed the rest of the night knowing it was Christmas Eve as that father would put up the tree with the beautiful lights. Still little scared to go to sleep at night I asked God to keep my siblings and me safe. Then it happened I woke up to Christmas and ran downstairs to see what my siblings and me had under the tree. My brothers and sister were already up and Jevone handed me my gift. I opened it and saw that it was a remotecontrolled car that made me so happy. I shared it with my siblings as our parents came down saying, "Merry Christmas," it was nice to see for a change and we really enjoyed that first Christmas at that house. That father bought mother an outfit set and they were enjoying each other company with them being a safe peace time together in a long, long time and with my siblings and me too, Thank You Jesus!!!

A few days later when we went back to school, we had a better feeling of Christmas as other kids were talking and showing off their Christmas gifts but I didn't really know anybody to share so I stayed to myself. It was another short week with New Year's Eve and we had early release once again. Running home with my brothers to the house as we all just took our bookbags off ran downstairs to watched

TV as our parents had their own TV upstairs in their room. It was a peaceful, safe, and relaxing and we still had a chance to go outside and play in the fresh snow. It was fun for a few hours and then other kids came out that we knew from neighborhood that we all played football in the snow. We then heard mother calling us to come on in for us to celebrate New Years' Eve. I was hoping and praying that God would keep this family loving each other into the new year as our parents decided to get up watch the party on TV with my brothers, sister and me watching shows like the Mr. Mikel Show. It was nice and as it became 11 p.m., I was excited to see we was going to make it through another year in one piece with less than fifteen minutes later, mother poured champagne for herself and that father, we had soda as mother gave a toast and kissed that father. We ended the night with a family hug saying "Happy New Year" 1983.

What a nice peaceful weekend into the New Year 1983 was here and my brothers and me got happy dress Monday going back to school and none of us were afraid. We just kept to ourselves and concentrated on our class work and with happy times this went on for several months. My challenging work and concentration paid off as I would be moving to the next grade level the following school year.

As the weeks and months went by good for the family as May ended and June was here, an easy month to go before finish school I felt good with great news of passing with C's and B's while my brothers did even better with A's and B's.

Staying to myself helped me from being picked on by kids though I know I looked weird with my big forehead that when I would walk through the hallway, I had my head down a lot and heard comments made about me but kept going.

That father was home one day when I came home from school with my brothers. It was Wednesday, two days before weekend as he was at the door asking what we were so happy about and I just said we got one more week before we were out of school. He just looked at me saying "yeah" and reminded me that I barely passed but ignored him went to my room.

There times he would come down steps say turn TV down its too loud and stuff like that so we had to walk softly each and every time during those weeks into July which still was my birthday month on the 23rd. . I was still terrified of him hurting me or touching me and did all I could to stay on his good side.

The weeks kept going by and we stayed busy keeping out of our parent's nerves as mother was still working a lot. Then my special day came it was my birthday waking up happy and went downstairs to see a cake for me too. I was fifteen and had made it this far, later my brothers came down singing Happy Birthday to me and hit me in the arm 15 times gently of course. Then Bernadette hugged me saying it too as mother came down to kiss me to see a very joyous day.

7

BACK TO OLD
THINKING

The summer was flying by fast with us all staying home. As boring as the summer was the only bright spot was our neighborhood friends that made us forget what we been through in recent years past. As August began to get hot out, we would still try to have fun outside and attempt to be quiet once we came inside of the house. However, on one occasion, we were excited about winning the neighborhood football game and we woke up that father and he showed us how much he didn't like us waking him up by his punishment we never forget.

I then started to have problems with my bowls again with it so hot outside and we didn't have an air conditioner in the house was a problem. One day on the weekend Saturday that father was washing clothes and found my dirty draws in the afternoon yelling telling me to come to basement. He grabbed me pulling my dirty draws up in my face showing me that they were so dirty and he couldn't clean them with the rest of the clothes. I just stood there knowing this was bad for me now as he sent me to my room saying wait for him then crying like a baby as my brothers just looked at me asking why I was so upset. I just ran into my room while they were downstairs watching tv that it wasn't good for them to be in that room with me as I was scared and crying.

Then that father came up the steps and he bust through the door telling me come in his room with the belt in his hand I just kept saying sorry. I had done well all this time and it was just an accident but he didn't want to hear it and started telling me take my pants down. I kept my draws on and begged my that father to forgive me but he didn't want to hear that. My brothers heard me crying and screaming but couldn't help me as he told me stand in corner and don't move. When he touched me inappropriately with his hand as I still was not moving just crying sorry but he said he loves me and didn't want to hurt me. Standing in that corner seemed like days as I said okay I sorry pushing him off and pulling my pants up running out of his room into mines slamming door tired of the abuse that I later fell asleep without even enjoying rest of that day or eating dinner. Thru the weekend and couple days I come straight to my room not even talking to my brothers covered up in the sheet staying in my bed for days only coming out to eat and went back to my room as my body was sore.

Mother didn't even care that I was not coming out of my room that one day woke up as it was Friday the last week in August, I was washing up but not really wearing my draws because too scared messing them up as that father came in bathroom asking me if I was ok saying he still loves me. Too disgusted with him touching me inappropriately, didn't want to even look at his face but he came at me saying change your look and stop being in the room all the time and go outside to play and I ran out so quick just sat on the front steps just to get away from all his abuse done to me in that house.

Later that day my brothers wanted to go outside and play but still not feeling up to it as Jevone kept asking me if I was okay just said not really but still went outside with them just to find some peace.

Still getting little nervous now that going in the 10th grade was more pressure of kids picking on me because I didn't talk or joke around in class and was the quiet kid.

The day after Labor Day my brothers and I were running like we were in track to get to school on time.

Our parents never helped us in the morning at all so we did our best as for me I just paid attention to the teacher and tried not to be the joke for all the kids that often laughed at me because of my big head or poor clothing.

A good thing that happened was that my younger brother Jevone was put into my same history class. There were issues with the school finding classroom for him so it was great to see him and sit together. However, we were both picked on by a loud mouth kid and he started to sit near us and was picking on me and the clothes Jevone and I wore.

When it was over Jevone was mad and we both got him in the corner of the class and Jevone yelled at him to immediately stopped picking on me that made it great to have Jevone in same classes together.

As the weeks of October weather started to change it was still nice out even though it was heading to fall. One day coming home from school I saw this nice, pretty girl walking past my block. Before she could get too far just said hi and then it happened, she stopped and turned around saying hi back. I never had gotten this far with a girl so didn't know what I should do next except stare at her. She then came toward me and started talking to me and asked me what my name was Maxine then she said bye and I was in shock like I couldn't move. Going into the house was a happy feeling that Jevone and Terance started asking me what happened. I said a girl said hi to me and went to my room smiling for a while into the house that day.

So, I started feeling little happier and not thinking I was an ugly looking kid. On Friday night Jevone and I went outside that evening to play catch football when I saw Maxine on her steps talking to another girl. So nervous still walked over there said hi as she said hi back and then she introduced me to her girlfriend name Ricky and I introduced them to my brother Jevone. As we stood there talking a little, I heard this loud voice yelling our names and it was that father telling us to get home. That was so embarrassing like we little kids so we both left in a hurry with our heads down.

With looking so mad on what that father did to us made it harder to go outside sometimes as fall weather here. It was starting to get cold outside so throughout the weekend we decided to hide in the house. On Saturday, Terance and me was coming home from the store for my parents and Maxine saw me walking she said hi. I was glad she still wanted to talk to me after that incident. She immediately told me not to worry about what happened and that she would talk to me more later. Eventually I had to find a way to still see her so Jevone and I would go outside to play with the other kids and then walk over to Maxine's steps and talk so our parents wouldn't embarrass us again. It worked for a few times until one day that father was looking for us, yelling our names loudly as we left the girls saying bye and running home quickly. We got in the house and he slammed the door asking what took us so long and I said just play. That father then said was it some girls because they are fast and will be trouble but I just went to my room and ignored him as Jevone did too.

The next day I saw Maxine outside with her girlfriend she still wanted to talk to me so she handed me her phone number and I was so happy almost couldn't talk!

Going back home, I was still in shock and happy that nothing could get me upset. But later I took a chance and knowing the danger had to ask my that father can I use the phone to call a buddy lying when wanting to call Maxine but still he said why should I do that, so I just said wanted a friend to talk, plus all you done to me was my first time speaking up that father got scared and agreed saying I had to do extra chores once was off the phone. I was allowed 30 minutes to talk to her with mother little mad saying why you let him use the phone but he had no choice of the abuse he done to me. So, I was in the basement steps with door closed happy kid called Maxine and she answered saying who is this and I told her it was me. She was happy to hear from me but I was so nervous for five minutes didn't know what to say. Finally, she started talking to me as I was just saying okay and she asked me what I like to do and then started to talk back a little that's when that father knocked on the door, opening it saying time to get off and she heard it and embarrassed me again ruin my night.

While my brothers were in the kitchen, they saw my expression and began laughing at me but it wasn't funny at all. Mother said she was listening in on my conversation too and said that whoever that girl is not good and they bad for you to be talking to. I just ran into my room so upset that again my family not only ruined my friendship with Maxine now I can't even focus on school.

As the days was getting colder and it was Halloween, I went out a little but not much. One day, Maxine was outside coming home from school and we talked a little but did not have that opportunity very often but I still was thankful just to say hi to her.

The school months went by fast as it was time for teacher conference meeting for that father to come to my school meeting that Wednesday. That father went and when he found out that I had a D in English class he was mad and embarrassed me. Once we were home, told me I would be getting a beating for the bad grade in English class. However, he told me if I did something for him then he wouldn't beat me or tell mother. Until then he just stayed away from me as rest of the week went on, I was trying so hard to do better in classes and study and scared of that father too. Every day after school I went right to my room got on my knees and prayed, asking God to please protect me and get me through all these nightmare abuses. Hoping God keep that father from wanting to touch me inappropriately and beat my siblings too.

Toward end of that week one night when everybody slept that father came into my room as I had my sheet wrapped tight around me saying I better improve on my classes or else and knew I need to pray for God to help me even more.

For weeks I would do my homework and study each night with tears running down my face. It was the first week of November getting colder but I was doing better in school but not good enough so I was still extremely nervous.

Then scared and having trouble with kids making fun of me at school I tried my best to ignore them but they just called me names like big head and all I could do was laugh with then instead of crying in classes only to get thru those school days. Into the weekend on Saturday night when it was time to go to bed and I slept but was coughing and needed to get some water downstairs. It was dark down there and no lights were on. That father was asleep on the couch So, I was trying to run back upstairs as he said to me that I owed him. I said please not now then he said I protected you from mother and punishment telling me if I don't do what he asked he would leave this family for good and never come back. Worried of his threats just let him touch me inappropriately standing behind me then that father pulled on me and I felt something else touching me inappropriately as he put his hands over my mouth and saying be quiet trying to push me on couch as I finally fought back saying stop it. Then I heard someone in the hall so he pushed away from me as I was pulling my pants up and ran up the steps into my room while Terance was in the bathroom curling up in my bed crying asking God to please, please help me falling to sleep in tears.

Thru the rest of the weekend, I didn't leave my room with that my safe place or go downstairs to eat anything as that father came in my room saying he was sorry and that he loved me. Still didn't believe him angry and upset ignored him with my back toward the wall in the bed because I couldn't look at him as a that father but a stranger trying to continue hurting me. Mother then came later in the room bringing me food and water saying I had to eat so a little of something but went back to sleep until dinner time. Still nervous and upset kept waking up afraid that father was going to sneak into my room later into the day but, found a way continue praying to God protect me going to sleep.

The next day I was tired but safe and glad to get out of the house away from that father on last day Sunday that weekend. My stomach problems were worse due to the stress and trauma at home so I didn't want to go back inside for a while.

With next week being Thanksgiving I wasn't feeling thankful and my health was getting worse with me constantly tired because I was scared to go to sleep at night.

As Thanksgiving was here our parents cooked a turkey and I came downstairs for breakfast to eat. I saw sweet potatoes and mashed ones made up with boxed stuffing and felt better to eat later that day as we gathered around the kitchen table having some type of Thanksgiving dinner unlike a civil family. It was good until that father did some fake praying that I couldn't even agree with just want some peace eating dinner.

On November 27th mother bought us winter coats out because it was cold out as going to school continued to be okay trying my best to ignore the teasing kids would do towards me in each classes.

The second week of December that father brought up the Christmas tree from the basement but had my brothers and me put it all together were that was the only time it was happy during that week project for us. We worked on decorating the tree and hanging up other decorations all week with our family Christmas tree being the prettiest on our block.

Those next couple of days were as that father was running around with mother doing their last- minute shopping making it better and safer for me that he was leaving me alone lately as well which was helping my health.

As going to school safer weeks went by in December for me, Thank God that I didn't even pay attention to next couple of days was Christmas. So, with me doing my last two days with it Christmas Eve my brothers and me got out of school early and was so, so happy that we all ran home wanting to just play and watch TV. With that father and mother home from we wanted to hurry up and eat so we go to sleep ready for Christmas. Then that blessing day came Christmas Day morning where my brothers, sister, and me all ran downstairs. My present was a new pair of pants and a hat and glove set as my siblings liked their gifts too. The day went well and I thanked God that He had heard my prayers and answered protecting my brothers, sister, and me on Jesus Christ Birthday.

That father was telling everyone Merry Christmas trying to be a fake and nice for a change but my siblings and me found a way together laughing and hugging each other. The weekend was peaceful with us playing outside then putting together our toys that we didn't want the happy weekend to end to going back to school. Still, not ready to head back to school but happy to show off my Christmas gifts of pants and gloves. It was a very relaxing time and I hoped the next year was going to be one full of less harm towards me and the rest of my siblings.

8

BIRTH OF NO FOUNDATION

The weeks went by ok with it becoming a week before New Year's Eve as I acted the same way heading into the new year January 1984, wanted to leave a lot of things behind me and start fresh as we woke up the next day to a chilly winter weather but quietness was good to have a peace of mind that day.

While we were sitting quietly watching the parades on TV me and my brothers had decided to go in our rooms. I was hiding my dirty drawers from my that father but my brothers were not exactly clean so the smell was not just from me. That father came up yelling for us to be quiet and thankfully he didn't notice the smell.

Each day after that it continued the same with my parent's temporary love and then going back to their old ways. As I continued to keep to myself together also found myself praying more. Friday came and it was supposed to be getting ready for New Year's Eve but didn't feeling well and had stomach issues. I was trying to wipe my body best could with me still too scared to go into the school bathroom. So, I stayed in my room for New Year's Eve slept thru the night and with my siblings up with mother and that father watching TV with countdown from 5,4,3,2,1 all I heard was Happy New Year but I didn't have much to celebrate just the same pain New Year 1984. I felt safer staying in bed getting ready the next day for school that Monday. As I got myself together in my safer cave ready to go to a less dangerous place at school with my brothers was little better. But made it thru my first day and left school running almost leaving my brothers behind. Kids were calling me stinky when that father came to me that night saying the room stunk. He opened the window and was looking at me then went behind the door and found my dirty draws saying you're in trouble. All I could say was sorry it was an accident and tried to keep them clean but the teacher didn't let me go to the bathroom so I started crying like because didn't want that father to touch me. Jevone and Terance soon came up asking what was wrong upset told them I messed up my draws and that father found it and was in trouble. Soon mother was yelling at me saying she was tired of my dirty draws and put me on punishment not to watch TV for a month.

Each day came home and did homework then she hit me saying I stink and was too old to be messing up my draws. She hit me over and over and once she left my room, I just cried my way through the rest of that night and didn't even get to eat. That father came back later, saying I'll teach you a lesson, as he hit me with the belt once, then twice crying in the corner. He was about to hit me a third time but stopped touching me inappropriately saying he loves me and didn't want to hurt me. He was still touching me inappropriately as he pulled on me too. Then finally stopped when mother knocked on the door and opened it, he hit me once more.

I couldn't even sleep was so, so scared he would hurt me again so for rest of that weekend I was so stressed and not talking at all not even to my brothers. Just stayed in my room only came out go to the bathroom then back to my room staying there, didn't even care about eating too scared to go outside the room, so it's my safe place.

With Monday here toward the end of the January going to school and dealing with my abuse issues from that father at home tried my best putting toilet paper inside my draws not to mess them up. At school I was still nervous as ever and the same classmates were still calling me "the skinny bigheaded boy" and "stink boy." I just wanted to hide but couldn't even do that at home. All the stress was still causing me to mess my pants up daily.

By the time school was over I had homework to do and was running home praying that life would be soon be better for me. Once got home it was the same thing just a different day. That father was looking at me coming in house asking if I had any accidents in school and looked at him, said no, went upstairs to my room with my brothers and continued to pray. Throughout the rest of February and March my focus was not the homework or the students but my draws. It got so bad for me one day I wore two pairs of pants so nobody smelled it, however, in class kids started to smell me sweating instead and I asked to be excused to the bathroom to clean up my up my draws.

By the time my parents returned home that evening, I was in my room and heard them come in. That father immediately burst into my room asking what you doing and I said just doing my homework then he went behind the door to see if there was any dirty draws, but he didn't see anything and then mother came in from work was my way of escape from him thank God.

The next couple of months at school I had to deal with a bully named Jeff. He kept pestering me in class so I was going to tell the teacher but knew that would just be more trouble. Did that once before and he beat me up. Instead, just waited until after class acting as though I needed help with the subject and told the teacher. The teacher said she would watch out for me that it made me see she was a blessing from God.

Knowing how much I been dealing with in the last 2 months left May and June just passed eleventh grade barely made me feel I accomplished something great during the trials been going through.

With summer almost arriving again and feeling breathe of relief and release the pressure out of school. I was looking forward to nights of TV and days playing outside with my brothers we decided to kick off the summer with a game play catch. The girls in our neighborhood were out too but I wasn't bold or confident enough in myself to talk to them. We were enjoying our summer each day just going outside not staying in the house.

As summer continued, no abuse took place and my birthday next week in July hoped it would be the best birthday and summer ever. Just doing everything I could to not get into trouble with my parents and straighten up the house, my room and even tried to do dishes. Also made sure no messed up my draws.

Finally, it was my birthday woke up to my brothers singing "Happy Birthday" and playfully punching me in my arm 16 times. My little sister Bernadette said it to me too and that was cute; mother kissed me and last came that father. He wished me good wishes with a smile and hugged me like he had never hugged me before but knew it was all fake. Still, I was given new clothes and a big breakfast of my favorite cereal and bacon, which normally we did not have. The rest of the day was good too that I was able to relax, and mother bought me a cake with 16 candles on it. The summer was good for me and felt safe as this feeling continued into the new school year of September toward me continue praying God get me thru that the safe days turned into weeks, months that Christmas in December was like just another day towards New Year's Eve with less abuse. I was hiding every chance could and making sure no more messing up my draws and keeping my eyes slightly open praying, asking God for happier times into 1985

9

THE BROKEN DREAM

The year of 1985 was my year of wholeness that I slept without bad dreams and did much better in school. Having no bullies to worry about at school and peace at home helped me so much that I made it thru the beginning of January to June passing to the next grade 12th with a C- average. It was enough to finally see how God heard my crying prayers of how that father has been treating me and my family that for us to really see peaceful loving safe times treating each other right.

As each day went by, I got through my classes with no problems and the next thing it was already the end of October 1985. Still wasn't having any problems with my stomach and very thankful my body was healing plus that father wasn't bothering me. Soon it was Thanksgiving then Christmas. I had made a new friend that really appreciated me. Her name was Kim and saw past my family life and saw my heart that we talk sometimes from her down the block of the neighborhood that she liked me and wanted to be more than friends but was just too scared to go down that path with my family so we still just remained good friends instead.

Things were getting a little bad between Terance and that father because they would argue alot about him getting a job to help the family. Terance would always argue with our parents a lot that it finally came down to Terance and that father having a fistfight. The fight was so bad that Terance knew he had to leave for a bit. He ended up going into the basement with me as I convinced him not to leave the house completely.

By the time we all calmed down it was later in the morning Terance slept in the basement and stayed there while mother was trying to keep the peace.

By that time in December Christmas was here with nothing different to celebrate as things went from good to just bad all the way around. The only thing I was happy about was my report card. Getting mostly C's and a B in math. However, this didn't please my parents as they yelled at me calling me silly. It hurt me so much that just couldn't wait for this Christmas and New Years to be over so was looking forward to a new year and leaving in 1986 to escape from that father abuse as a senior and potentially move out soon.

January went by it was the middle of February and the school teacher of English and History told me that if I didn't get higher grades in these two classes wouldn't graduate. My heart sank knowing I had to pray and do my absolute best. Once home went upstairs sitting there crying myself to sleep for better tomorrow. The next day got up and was determined to do my best to graduate then try to leave this abused home environment. So, during the last class of the day I met a new girl named Tamika and all the sudden we just instantly started talking as she asked me if I was going to prom and told her no didn't have a date, neither did she. So, we exchanged numbers then talked all rest of the week at school about going together and she would provide the transportation too that event made my entire day better.

Then came the moment that made me scared and nervous but had to go asked my parents that weekend in the morning went upstairs to my parent's room and asked them could I go to my prom telling them I had a date with Tamika from school as they both were shocked. Mother said okay but who is she and how you going to get there, so told them again she goes to my school and she would provide the transportation so they agreed. I ignored my parents and still was excited and happy calling Tamika as we talked and planned it out. It was my first date ever on a prom as my parents gave me money telling me to go down to Sizton Store to rent a suit.

Weeks went by fast with me busy doing everything I could keep my grades good in school getting my prom suit then praying thanking God kept me safe at home. Finally, the day arrived and it was prom night I was so happy and excited that got my haircut looking nice as my brothers and sister were happy for me too. Mother took our picture but that father said nothing as I kept smiling then the doorbell rung and it was Tamika as mother took a picture of us both then we left in her car joyful day for me off to prom! Once we got there the school looked nice and we had an enjoyable time. As soon as it was over, Tamika said she had plans for us to go to an after the prom to party. We were out past midnight, and we had a great night! She even gave me a kiss on the cheek goodnight dropping me off to home. When I knocked on the door that father greeted me at the door and asked did I have a fun time. I said yes, went upstairs and happily went to sleep safe as that father was still mad he couldn't get his way with me God protected me this time.

The weekend came it was so great to wake up Saturday with my nice prom night out that it made my weekend so much better. Then later asked my parents could I call Tamika just to talk to her as mother was like no but that father said okay, just know with him it's consequences. So still happy used the phone called Tamika said did you have suitable time she said yes and ask could we see each other again but she said has a boyfriend. She said she would rather just be friends and that was fine with me just at least I have somebody to say hi to as school. Later that day I had to return the tuxedo before we were charged extra. It was a nice ride there on the trolley and then walked around down town for a while enjoying myself and the day of safe happiness.

That night was much different though as I was sleeping that father hit me telling me come downstairs now about my dirty draws that he found them in basement and said he going tell mother so I went to get them. Then walking to living room he was on the couch crying saying mother didn't love him anymore and he wants to leave the family and I said don't do that. Next thing he asked me could he just see my body or he leaving family for good wanted to tell him no but he got angry threatening to leave us be with another woman. I was so scared of what he said and thinking about Kevin and Bernadette just cried again pulled me into the corner room. He started to touch my body then pulled on me and pushed me on the couch. He had my face in the couch so and I couldn't scream, then tried to molest on me. I pushed him off with my arms angry telling him stop it hurts as someone was walking to the bathroom and he got off me. I ran upstairs fixed my pants up as my brother was in bathroom and curled under my covers balled my fist screaming into the pillow wanting to hurt that father but knowing God gave me another way of escape thru another nightmare.

Waking up still angry nothing to smile about just continued to hide in my room mad that my happy weekend had been ruined and was still in pain from the abuse.

Monday morning so tired and upset ran to school and remembered there was an important test in history class to take but know I did study for it because this was my last chance to pass 12th grade. Still nervous taking the test but felt I did good too as after class was over the teacher told my grade was a 91 on my history test, so feeling happy knowing that last week I also got a 90 on my English test too. These two classes I needed to pass to graduate praying this will be enough.

As I was so happy outside of school over waiting for Jevone we laughed and had fun as he told me he passed all his classes too to 12th grade so it was happy times going home. Once me and my Jevone came home from school that father was there at the door looking at me as if he needed to speak with me. He told me the school called and said the rest of my grades were too low to graduate. Not listening shocked thinking he was lying since I passed both my English and

History tests with 90 and 91, but still about to cry like just ran upstairs to my room upset with no words to say anything. Terance and Jevone just tried to talk to me but it wasn't enough as I kept crying thru that worst day of my life until falling to sleep.

Thru the next couple of days as Jevone went to school while Terance was looking for a job and I was so depressed that didn't want to go back to school for the last week of class and see the other kids happily graduating. It was the worst days of my life as Jevone came home from school saw me still in my room crying as that father told family I not graduating. Mother was upset and mad that she hit me with her hands saying you are silly and no summer for you as the rest of the night continued to cry my way thru it.

Later that morning after Jevone went to school for last week before his graduation and Terance out for a job mom at work and Kevin and Bernadette in their rooms, that father came Upstairs and told me to wake up and come into his room. I told him to leave me alone but he insisted with me so Upset and scared but went in knowing more pain and abuse. He told me mother was Upset with me and disappointed and that I needed to work on earning a GED this summer. He said that mother wanted to punish me for the whole summer but he said no except to owe him once again for this and knew what that meant.

Then he made phone calls and found out when summer school was while I was very afraid he would come hurt me anyway. Sure enough, with Kevin and Bernadette sleeping, he came in and told me to pull my pants down. And tried to abuse me again but this time fought back for the first time and yelling get off me or I tell mom and threatened him and swinging my left arm trying to hit him like never before. Finally pushed him away and ran while pulling my pants up. He then ran behind me but I shut the door and locked it before he could come in. As he tried to apologized thru the door all I could think of was wanting to punch, punch him over and over as many times he abused me. Then he walked away from the door as tears coming down my eyes in the bed just was asking, begging God praying PLEASE STOP HIM FROM ABUSING ME INTO ANOTHER SUMMER knowing I have no one else that can help me.

10

HANGING ON THE THRESHOLD!!

J evone and everyone else in neighborhood started to enjoy summer. As the weeks went by the day came when I had to begin my GED classes. Mother gave me money to catch the bus at Rectin Street by eight that morning. On my way to the bus stop, I asked God to help me get through this while getting on the bus ride still nervous but got there seeing a lot of kids from school going there that I thought should have graduated so it felt better not the only one. Taking my time then walking thru to the classroom noticed a girl I knew from school but didn't say anything except surprisingly she sat rite next to me.

Still trying to listen to the teacher I took notes and was determined to study hard for upcoming tests.

Finally, the day was good got out of school went home, had fell asleep knowing this is just the beginning have to finish strong get my GED diploma. Mother came into my room woke me up and started hitting me. She said to get up eat and told me I was not to watch TV that and not to shame the family by being unusual. She said that aside from eating and going to the bathroom I needed to stay in my room to focus on summer school.

So, trying to concentrate on my classes was still difficult with no new friends by myself. But I took a chance and saw that girl in my class named Evon so sat next to her. She said hi and I said hi back as we talked and it was okay that I felt better coming here for my GED. And thru the course of the summer months I got to have a nice friendship with Evon.

August came and I studied doing my best on my exams. Evon and I often discussed our classes to and from school on the el train. This helped and we were both able to pass our exams with high scores.

One night I was doing well, relaxing with my siblings, and watching TV. That father called me into his room and tried to tell me he missed me as I was about to yell but Bernadette came upstairs to her room and he left me alone. So tired of this abuse I continued to pray so much for God to please help me and protect me from my that father keep abusing me all thru rest of that night. The next day I woke up in so much pain in my body and started crying went into the bathroom. Mother asked what was wrong but I didn't answer as on the toilet my bowls had blood in them. I told mother my body hurt and she told me to drink more water. This was my last day of summer school and wanted it to be a good day not start out like this.

Still determined to get my GED was in pain drinking a lot of water got there as the teacher told everyone get ready for your test and with Evon sitting next to me as we both was nervous. So, the class took our test as I let class going home praying, I passed to move on and not be a unusual kid anymore with me still on punishment slept in my room thru the night. As God got me thru that night to see this last day of summer school, I got dress quick racing out the house praying God bless me with some good news. I saw Evon and she asked you think you did good and I hoped so. Then the teacher said congratulations everyone passed and handed us our certificates that I was so happy couldn't stop happy crying but not to look soft happy as Evon was too and we hugged leaving out. This was the best summer I never had with a new friend and cute girl, so the day had turned out great that God answered my prayers.

As I said bye to her and got home around 4pm happy and taking my time not in a rush to go back to the abused house that father questioned what took me so long so I told him we were saying goodbye since it was the last day and enjoying delightful day of us getting our GED as he still wasn't happy for me. But I still told mother and she was happy also my brothers and sister too that it was the best family time I ever had. So later enjoying fun time Nathen needed to tell me something so we met in the basement where he slept at and he told me he is leaving for the service in two weeks. I was so, so happy for him escaping but sad he must go out this way to escape and have his freedom and I am still stuck here not free.

The next couple days were quiet with Terance getting ready to be leaving for service just going to miss my big brother so we still got together for the last happy time out weekend all day on Saturday to play catch outside until it was dark. That father started calling us to come in block, yelling our names loud and all. We came in but still happy to have fun talking again like brothers and knowing this last time we play with Terance so ate and we went to sleep fine with another safe weekend for me while Terance was out enjoying his last few days. I was happy he was going to be able to leave but sad to see him go. With the weekend a safe one that Tuesday Terance said goodbye to us all mother, Jevone, Kevin, Bernadette, and me as we all cried wish he stay but he had to go and escape as that father acted like he didn't even care. So, he took his stuff mother still crying as he stood at the door and said love yall leaving for something better for his life.

In the middle of the night still upset Terance was gone out there into the service my stomach started hurting me again got me really praying for my family. All this time and all I had been through, still had faith that God would intervene.

Later, started to look for a job because I didn't want be in this house alone with that father. Had got dress early in morning to walk to the plaza and picked up applications so not to be around that abusive that father touching me. I applied at many places staying out all day that Jevone was home from starting 12th grade school and told him I had applied to Bunns Restaurant hoping they give me a chance to work and not be in the house of pain.

The next day going to the store for that father and found a job at Packers. They were looking for young men to unload trucks for $10 per hour. Hours were midnight to four in the afternoon and no experience was required and told that father I'm going to apply for this job the next day.

Extremely excited next morning got dressed to apply for the job. Went for a walk to catch the trolley down there and took the orange train, then walked ten blocks. Got down there at suitable time and filled out the application praying they would hire me.

Weeks went by when I was about to leave the house to apply for more jobs but that father scolded me about my dirty draws. He told me get my nasty draws together and come in his room with mother at work and Jevone, Bernadette and Kevin still sleeping. He told me no girl would want to be with me if I smelled all the time. I told him I was trying my best but had stomach problems but he said I need an enema and went to the store to get one knowing he just wants to abuse me but didn't want to be having accident trying get a job so took a shower and sat in my room scared waiting for him while Jevone woke up and said what's wrong. Told him I having bowl problems and that father went to the store get me enema to get my bowls rite. Then he came back as he told me go in bathroom and I was just praying asking God to please keep me safe as that father came back and put the enema in and out as it hurt so bad that I almost passed out crying and yelling that had my brothers and sister wondering was I okay as that father said yelling thru the bathroom door saying he is fine. Finally, he left me in bathroom for a while as I let all that bowls out in the toilet and so tired that almost fell asleep on the toilet but got up went rite to bed and slept the remainder of the day.

That next day slept off and on still getting up a couple of times going to the bathroom. Needed to rest because had a job interview in a few days. Later feeling better got it together dress up and went downtown to apply for a Riter Store job. I saw two girls in an ice cream store and one girl looked cute. After I picked up the application came back out hoping to see the girls. Later ended up talking to them and getting the cute girls' phone number!

I was so happy skipping home and smiling never had such a wonderful day. It got better once I got home because Packers called and wanted to interview me and immediately thanked the Lord.

So excited got off the phone went downstairs told that father I had a job interview at Packers. He had no support for me, but it didn't bother me. Just went to tell Jevone upstairs in our room and at least he was excited for me! Then mother came home and she was happy for me as well. She told me if to relaxed and you will do well don't be nervous for Mondays interview.

I slept so well that night that waking up the next day ready to get this new job this morning when that father came in mumbling about my drawers. Said to him not to touch me and slammed the door.

I did well at the interview and Packers hired me and ready for my new beginning.

11

WALKING
PATHWAYS

ent to bed early and slept well until I heard the alarm then got up dress and had car fare to catch the trolley but had to run all the way there not to miss it. So, out of breathe did make it on the trolley at 9:30pm happy staying awake until I got on the orange line train at Coconot and market and happy that I got to work at 11:55 pm, but out of breath told them my name and was put to work to unload a 18 wheeler of items back of the Packers trailor. The supervisor said I was doing well but needed to work a little faster. Being my first job did my best and had finished one to two trailors in 4hrs of time but was so, so tired heading back home ready to sleep like a rock.

Later, got home had a key to get in the house walk into the door while everybody was still sleeping and went safely to my room praying to sleep with no harm. It was the afternoon and God heard my prayers because nothing happened to me while I slept as Jevone came home from school waking me up. Told him my job is hard to unload 18 wheeler trailors by myself. Then he told me he had okay day at school as we relaxed and began talking about the new girl that I had met at the ice cream shop, Sosha. I wanted to talk to Sosha but had to discuss it with mother and that father before asking her out, however, Jevone didn't really want me to do that because he knew they would be against it.

Finally knowing the outcome still went to ask them both that night met someone nice her name is Sosha and could I call her. They both said no just like that and I went to my room so mad didn't eat dinner stayed in my room sleeping in anger. Then still went to work next day got home and while mother and Jevone wasn't home that father came at me. He woke me up from my sleep saying I will let you talk and see her if you do something for me and it was the same abuse nothing change. He pushed me into my room saying just stand in the corner to see Sosha and I believed he wouldn't hurt me but then that was a lie still was crying ready to yell and wake up Kevin and Bernadette but didn't want to scare them so I pulled me into the corner room. Still crying and scared he came up behind me touching my body asking if I get excited around her. Then he started in a inappropriate way and grabbed my body saying its okay.

Before he could abuse me again then I screamed and he stopped.

Pushing him off me running to my room and locked the door behind me just angry to myself thinking is a girl worth all this pain and abuse.

Doing my best through that month trying to work and avoid that father at the same time. However, things got bad that I lost my job because wasn't fast enough to unload the trailor.

So, a little upset about that but had some hope with Sosha as I sneaked a call her on the phone often when parents were in their bedroom.

A couple of weeks went by and then it was Thanksgiving. I called Sosha to wish her a Happy Thanksgiving quickly. I was happy to hear her voice as we talked but had 10 minutes before eating as we said bye to each other.

Then December was here and there was snow outside. I got my first check, which was $200 after tax and had to give the family half to help them pay bills they didn't pay so it left me with $100 as I still bought myself clothes and Jevone helped me pick out a scarf and glove set for Sosha.

Knowing it was Christmas week and I still didn't have much to be happy about as my parents putting up the Christmas tree and lights and had Bernadette helping. Later through the night it was peaceful and good waking up the next day to Christmas with snow outside. We opened the few presents we had and I called Sosha to tell her "Merry Christmas." Also asked her if I could stop by with her present as she said yes and I immediately got dress telling my parents. Though my parents were still a mess they let me go see her which was a shocker. So, got dress quick running over to her house as the that father opened the door saying "Merry Christmas." I was a little nervous but came into the house didn't stay long just for a little bit, telling them where I lived, how old I am and how many siblings too. Sosha parents kept their eyes on every word that came out of my mouth. Hoping not to stutter they ask me did I want something to eat as Sosha open her present. I politely declined and watched her open her gift. She liked the gloves and matching scarf said thank you and hugged me. I said it was nice to meet them said bye to Sosha hugging her and left out the house happy going back home. Once home my parents ask what happened I told them it was okay and that I met her parents and Sosha really liked the gift as well.

That day made the rest of my week great even though with my family I saw no Happy New Year just another up and down year. I thanked God for all He has done to protect me from worse things happening as well as that I now had someone that cared for me. As the New Year 1987 came, I felt things would turn out ok waking up thinking I should attend school to get a better job. So later that week called the PCC Institute near Dandler Street and asked what type of school they were. They told me they were a computer and business school. It sounded interesting to learn about computers as Mrs. Terry the coordinator told me how much tuition was, she also said I could qualify for financial aid. She suggested I come down and get paperwork and then told that father but he wasn't happy and I didn't' care.

The next couple days was getting ready happy for my interview at PCC Institute, however, my parents were upset that I lost my other job and we had a big argument over the whole thing.

That Saturday January 10th I decided to try to get my drivers' permit so that I could get to school and be able to drive to work. It made me nervous so needed to make sure to hide my dirty clothes well.

It still was a great weekend and I accomplished many things. Monday was my interview with the school, so I did laundry making sure to have clean clothes. I was thinking about Sosha and walked to the corner store payphone called her phone instead of being yelled at by my parents. It rung two times but then I was about to hang up as she said hello and I was so happy. We talked for a while about what I was up to and nice that Sosha was supportive.

When I got home saw Jevone and told him of my plan for bettering my future and man was he was supportive too as things were looking up it seemed.

12

FAMILY STARTS
AND I FINISH

I woke up, got dressed and was on my way leaving house the by 8:30am so I could catch the trolley and be on Dandler Street by 10 am. Got to my interview and took the test for one hour. They asked me questions and told me I did well and would be starting next Monday. Heading home with a bounce in my heart of this blessing opportunity God had given me to be learning about computers and business just as many college students were doing.

I got to the house and that father yelled at me wondering where I had been. Just told him went to my interview and showed him the papers for the computer school telling him they got me a grant for $1500 to start school next Monday. He said that was fine but I still needed a job during the day.

So anyway, stayed in my room, went to sleep it off but then later he bust in said he found my dirty draws. And said if I showed him my body, he wouldn't tell mother as I got angry saying leave me alone stop hurting me. He then started to get loud asking if I want to see that girl Sosha needed to do this for him. Then it happened balling my fist up about to punch that father but knowing I wanted to see Sosha my happiness I slowly crying and angry pulled me into the corner room to let him touch me inappropriately again. Then he stood up behind me inappropriately trying to upset me until I said please, please stop it or I am going to tell mom everything you done to me for years.

The next thing I did was pull my pants up ran back to my room locking the door behind me.

That night couldn't even sleep terrified and angry at that father wanting to hit and hit him so he can feel my pain of his abuse repeatedly.

Wednesday remained safe and when everybody was leaving and I kept that door locked for a couple of hours. At noon, the phone rang and that father said it was for me. I went to the kitchen and took the phone call and it was a temp agency, Career Temps, asking me could I come down for an interview next Tuesday at 11am for a position as a mail clerk. I said yes and hung up the phone with tears of joy in my eyes.

That Saturday I awoke and felt better about the week ahead of me. I even went outside and played football for most of the day.

Later, in my room had talked to Jevone about asking Sosha to be my girlfriend and he said that's nice but be careful you know our parents are not happy and will stop your happiness too but she is worth it.

I woke up thanking God for a momentous day with Tuesday came and was ready for a new job as that father tried to fake being nice wished me good luck.

The interview lasted four hours as I was nervous because had to take a typing test and a math. Then came the rest of the questions and answered telling them I used to work at.

Still at Packers job as I saw a hard worker unloading10,000 boxes of merchandise knew what I had to do but still happy leaving the interview with confidence to get the job and told and had to tell that father and mother it went well. Later went to bed early keeping my mind on computer class next Monday too that God is hearing my prayers as I went to sleep safer. Later still happy thinking about going back to school then waking up for a few minutes heard mother walking around getting dressed for work but went right back to sleep for hours. Still, something wrong again happened that father busted in the room waking up telling me to get up he needed me to be ready for the kids because he had to take care business. As he left, I could breathe again and was so relieved watching TV, then later after 2pm the doorbell rang and it was Jevone coming in from school he said he did well on his studies.

As everybody came home went into my room when the phone rang and that father came out of his room telling me it was for me. Running so fast almost fell, got the phone in the kitchen it was temp agency downtown. They told me that I did well on my test and the job at the bank needs somebody to work immediately next Monday from 8am to 4:30pm. I almost stopped breathing saying yes! I thanked them and hung up the phone so, so happy then telling everyone in the house that I got a job! Went running and kissing Kevin and Bernadette as they just looked at me as if I was. Jevone came out of his room and told him the good news too as he was happy.

That day was a wonderful day to be happy as I was about to start fresh with a new job as a temp at the bank. So excited about going back to school for more education in computers. My confidence was back and not a depressed young man though was still having bad dreams of that father touching me inappropriately.

13

LIVING LIFT ABUNDANTLY

Monday came and went and everything was going well that I happily slept all week.

Then Friday was here I woke up so full of good energy and realized it was time to learn how to drive to school. I called the Motor Vehicles Building asking them what I needed to study to pass the test. They said I needed to get the booklet from them so I left out to go pick up the booklet on my way to work.

My training continued and had one coworker train me throughout the week. It went well and I enjoyed it so far.

Later made it to my computer class on time walking through the front door, the receptionist told me to go to the second floor. Our teacher introduced himself and then we said our names. Everybody seemed nice and happy to be there as I took notes while the teacher explained how the class would be conducted. There were some older people in the class too but the atmosphere was promising.

A few hours went by and we then had 15-minute break but continued working on a computer and on a Windows System. The teacher explained other parts of computer programs and the business aspect as well. I had a good day on my first day at computer school and work. Got home at 10:30 pm and had to ring the bell because I didn't have a key. That's when that father hit me, reminding me all he had done for me with him upset I had woken him up but I still went upstairs not touched thank you Jesus. So next day woken up upset crying having a bad dream of that father touching me when Jevone came into the room, I just said it was just a bad dream and had to get focus on work and school can't stop now!

I went back to work as rest of the day was great; then it was time to go home but wasn't in a rush so walked around downtown a little more at Missap Street and went to a few stores. The first store I went to was the Fraiction Store looking at some clothes and couldn't wait for my paycheck to buy some. Then made it home Jevone open the door and we talked about how our day was.

As everybody slept, I crept downstairs looking for the leftover spaghetti in the refrigerator. Heading back to my room, that father came down the steps looking, asking what was I doing. Trying go by him he grabbed me and said he needed to talk to me about who Sosha was because she had called while still shocked couldn't answer but he asked again why she calling here but did remember telling her my number only call if I tell her to. I told him how nice she was but he didn't want hear that. He just yelled, telling me I was in trouble if mother found out. "So, you need to help me and I will help you." I tried to go by him saying "whatever." He then grabbed my body saying "I miss you." Then was about to go but said what a nut that father you are for doing this to me your son and he was speechless.

So then ran to my room wanting to throw the spaghetti at the wall but didn't want to wake the family. It's been so, so hard to keep all of this inside all these years painful sacrifice to protect my siblings from hurting that father. Just went to my room, angry until finally fell asleep with tears coming down my face. Next day I woke up still not happy upset from last night got dressed quickly and left for work.

After work headed to class as the teacher allowed us to get some reading done on our computer books. Once I got home mother had dinner for me was a pleasant change. Ate and went to bed with confidence and was looking forward to the weekend. However, my happiness was ruined because I came to work as my boss told me they had chosen my coworker for the permanent position and not me and was hurt all thru my last day there. Going home crying on the inside and tired of being disappointed every time.

I came home late to eat dinner and ate downstairs until it got late and everybody went to bed with that father looking at me like he wanted to touch me inappropriately again but I just yelled leave me alone!!

As mom woke up saying what's going on and that father lied saying he told me go to bed but I was still so upset all night room punching my pillow and the bed like it was his face for ten minutes then tiring out falling asleep. My whole week was depressing because of the job and that father but had one thing going for me was to stay focused on passing my test for computer school. Later thought of calling Sosha so went to a pay phone and called her and we talked for 30 minutes. It was nice too and she said she wanted to see me so we made a date.

Went to school and did well on my test to the best of my ability so finally got home and found out from mother she called the house and she was little upset saying who is this girl why she calling here. I told her she lives in the neighborhood nice person as she went to bed with that father upstairs not bothering me. So, I waited until hearing their door closed and called her see if she was still up as it was after 10pm. Sosha picked up the phone little tired but I said just calling to say goodnight and she said it back to me as that made my night better.

The weekend was nothing but seclusion in my cave room and couldn't wait for next Saturday when I had my date with Sosha as I told Jevone and he was happy for me but I needed him to go outside with me like we were playing together so he agreed. I did nothing but sleep and eat in my room keeping my mind on studying for class and see Sosha.

The week went by safe and okay as that Saturday finally came as me and Jevone told parents we going outside to play and Jevone waited in the park as I went to her house while her parents were out at the store, rang the doorbell and she let me in quickly as I sat down and we talked about her family. It was a precise time and then she told me she smoked cigarettes but had stopped. She asked me to go upstairs to her room and I started to sweat and couldn't breathe saying nothing but followed her and saw her room for five minutes then left quickly back down the steps and said it was nice seeing you. I did ask her if she had a girlfriend we could introduce to my brother as she said yes, the one I had seen at the ice cream so we planned to set that up later.

I left and waved bye to her running back to the park where Jevone was waiting for me. Told him I had had an enjoyable time and that I may have found him a girl for him to talk to.

The next week I was learning more in my classes such as elements of Microsoft and Windows and passed my quiz with a good grade, a B-.

I also got to talk to Sosha on the phone for a bit in the hallway outside my class and talking with her motivated me. I kept going like a train through the months and went to school making it to the month of May. Jevone was talking about going to his prom because he had a date with a girl in his class as All in all, things were going well.

14

BREAK OF
CHAIN CYCLES

oming back home to the house and that father was in living
room tried to talk to me I just said all loud leave me alone and
went to my cave room. Sleeping through that night with no
reason to come out to check up on anybody. As the weekend past
I did nothing but sleep making it safely to Monday afternoon and
looked forward to class and a phone call with Sosha.

My week went okay and was feeling better while Jevone was
learning how to drive. The phone rang and that father said it was for
me and took it found out I got a job at Bunns Fast Food letting me
know I be a cook there. So, then hung up so happy running upstairs
telling that father as he just said okay but Jevone was happy then later
told mom she was too and thought about all my prayer talks to God
were heard thanks be to God.

That next morning woke up full of joy and got dress for class but
leaving out hugged Jevone, Kevin, Bernadette, and mother with so
much joy that God had brought back into my life. By the time I got
to school was talking to my classmates about my new job and knew
had to tell Sosha soon with me having an exciting time in class then
heading home.

Woke up the next day happy knowing I had plans to see Sosha and ask Jevone about how his driving training with that father was going and said it was good except that father was a little grumpy.

I called Sosha and she answered telling her I missed her also I have a new job at Bunns and she was so happy for me asking when she would meet my parents but said not sure.

Later, I relaxed in my room with Jevone and we just talked and then went to bed early.

It was Monday the end of August at 6:30 am waking up and got ready for the day and went to new job got there started received orientation.

My first day was okay as they had me work immediately in the kitchen and it went well even though it was quite hot in the kitchen. I left happy and glad to be working again and headed to school but smelling a little like chicken. As I got to school and continued my work week everything was going well and thanked God.

It was a busy day and people packed into the restaurant like. I had to hurry but be careful of the hot grease when dumping fries to be cooked and didn't want to get burned. Time flew by but got to school found out I had B in class and was thankful for it.

Then got home and slept like a baby having no conversation with anyone just looking forward to a peaceful weekend hoping to see Sosha. I couldn't complain with my stomach better and not messing up my draws that much either. The weekend was good and Jevone and I stayed outside playing football even though the weather was cooler and still got a chance to see Sosha where we met me at the park telling me she missed me and I told her the same. However, she still wanted to meet my parents and I couldn't resist her saying okay as we kissed and cuddled. It was a wonderful time and we were together for a while then it was time to go. As we left, I walked her to the corner of her house said bye and felt so lucky as me and Jevone went back into house knowing God is still giving us happy safe times.

So still scared for Sosha to meet my parents had to still ask so I went upstairs to mom and that father asking them could Sosha meet yall she wants to and mom said no but that father for his gain said yes knowing the consequences all I went thru suffering pain and abuse. So, we set it up for the week for her to meet them but I was praying that God keep them respectful and not lose Sosha.

As the week was okay, we had been cleaning up the house and for that day on Wednesday when Sosha coming over I got up and straighten my room and cleaned the bathroom and the rest of the house. I didn't want Sosha to come into a sloppy house as I cleaned for a while mopping and my parents didn't help but called her as she was going to come over after church.

I got myself dressed in a nice outfit telling my parents she said okay and mother decided to make her dinner as well.

Once that day came rang the doorbell and I opened it saying hi to her as she came into the house. As she arrived the family was excited and talked to her about a variety of subjects including asking her about her family. She was a little nervous but handled my mom and that father okay then talked to Jevone about her friend wanting to meet him and he blushed. After a while it was time for her to go and was so glad that she didn't leave with the messy questions she had to deal with. Asking how long she lived her what school she going to do she have smoke and stuff but she still left with a smile as I walked her home happy and I kissed her goodnight on the porch.

The new week was happy one and then in the mail we received a letter from Terance and he told us he was staying at the Cendwood for Thanksgiving with his fiancé and we all were shocked knowing if it's true or not at least he is not stuck here still in this abusive family.

I just continued to work, went to school each day, and talked to Sosha. Each time we talked she motivated me and then time passed by that it was Christmas time. She even came to my job and once it was my break time so I kissed her saying Merry Christmas. She said she wanted to surprise me and had my present was coming after work to surprise and see me to exchanged gifts there. So, still at while all my coworkers Sosha came in at job and we hugged and I kissed her as she looked and I was so happy but then had to get back to work as she gave me gloves and scarf and she liked the sweater I gave her. We hugged kissed and I went back to work feeling this was the best

Christmas I had ever had. Then headed home and everybody was up seeing the tree and then went to bed happy.

That Thursday night I had no school so after work changed my clothes then came over to Sosha parent's house nervous, scared, and shy but had to do this to make Sosha happy. It went well and the night was actually fun as I thanked God for this huge blessing!! And later finish the year strong with a normal but different feeling Happier New Year knowing I leaving this one with extra happiness to take with me into the New Year!!

15

DAYDREAM
WAKENING!!

Waking up to something new with support from God and Sosha was great as Monday, January 1st I went to work had to be there 8 am. Knocking back door the manager had me cleaning the back room up. Later I went to school and made it to class and the teacher was teaching us more about Windows 95 and how to navigate through and practiced using Excel well too.

At home I sneaked to call Sosha and talked to her for a little bit saying that I am falling for her and she thought that was sweet but didn't say anything more.

Later having a good working week Friday was here with me able to see Sosha more and by the end of the week we introduced her friend to Jevone. That weekend I told Sosha I loved her and she said she loved me too as rest of the weekend was good with Jevone applying for a job at Woolworths.

Happy going to work on that Monday I realized it was close to me graduating from my computer course.

Later went home scared and nervous having to talk to that father about having sex with Sosha knowing the danger of it as he went off saying you already did it but I told him no and wanted to know about getting gifts. We talked more but had to stop because Jevone came home so we waited until later next day when everyone was in bed knowing is this information worth being touched all over again. During the week that father came at me when I was in my room alone as Jevone was at work and he tried to touch my pants and I said loud, no, no more. He got mad as mom came in hallway asking what's wrong and he lied saying he was telling me to clean my room up knowing I finally spoke up.

The next day still scared came home from new job happy as that father tried to talk to me pointing at my body saying that is how you have precise time and I just said okay now leave me alone and ran up the steps to my room locking the door for the rest of the night. With this the last weekend of January, I still went to work and school the teacher told the class we all will be graduating. I was so excited and called Sosha and she was so happy for me said she loves me as I said love you too and we hung up.

As Valentines' Day was coming, I gave my that father money to buy mother something, I was going to buy something for Sosha too looking forward to showing love to her as she brought me so much caring happiness.

Weeks went by and then that special day came Valentine's Day and I called Sosha to Say Happy Valentine's Day and she said it back to me too. Just asked could I drop off her gift, Mom and that father said yes, so later as my family did give mom some flowers for Valentine's Day. I then got dress and ran all the way up to Sosha house got there rang the doorbell. Her that father came to the door and I said hello Mr. Wilson it's Daire can I come in I have a Valentine's Day Gift to give to Sosha as he slowly opened the door letting me in. I said hi to Her mother and happy Valentine's Day to her then Sosha as she came down the steps and gave her the heart candy and a card and we talked a little. She then gave me a kiss on the cheek and I said thanks while her parents went to the basement. I kissed her a lot more on the lips and we had to do it quickly because I couldn't stay long. Finally, said goodnight to her parents and Sosha walked me to the door as she kissed me again then we said goodnight and was so happy just singing all the way home. As the week continued with happiness me going to graduate that I woke up to the final day of school and Sosha called to tell me congratulations. I was happy told her it's been long road but I didn't quit and she agreed.

Then had to go ask that father about going out with Sosha to the movies he just said okay, with nothing asking in return as I thank God. I quickly got dress left out and hook up with Sosha as we met to go out.

We had an exciting time going out downtown and came back at a reasonable time as we kissed goodnight in front of her house and I went home so happy and thankful to God for this time together with her.

At home knowing I needed to talk to that father about having safe sex but was nervous to do so with his up and down abuse. Instead, the family talked about Terance and how he was going to leave the service to get married so that kept me going to bed safe as my parents were concerned about him.

The next day it was time to head to work and I was doing well at the job and had been there for six months. I took each day and each week in stride. Sosha and I were still together, then one day during the week she met me at the park one night. We were talking and she said she wanted to have enjoyable time and wanted to plan a day as I was speechless but nodded my head yes.

I had to go speak with that father about sex and gifts as he came into my room closing the door, I told him Sosha and me want to have precise time and we love each other. Then he said we need to talk more because we need to know what we are doing so that I did not get her pregnant. At first, he wanted me to please him but I convinced him not to thank God and instead we just talked.

That night was the most dangerous sacrifice part of my life for love as that father was still mad that I stop him from touching me as he asked and I said no I tell mom bailing my fist and went rite to my room almost hitting him.

That Friday I woke up so upset from the bad dreams of that father's awful suggestion and stayed outside not coming straight home from work until everybody was there. Went to my room hiding thru the weekend to myself praying to get thru to still see Sosha.

Finally, Monday morning came and had the day off and a date with Sosha. Left out of the house for that special day with her and went to ring the doorbell excited but nervous too. I was still happy as she opened the door looking nice with her rob on and we went Upstairs to her room. She lay me down on her bed and started to kiss me.

Still nervous though we tried to have wonderful time together but then nothing happened and was scared as she was mad at me saying what's wrong and I said never done this before. She started yelling at me and told me to go home as I left her house crying all the way home with nothing to be happy about again. Coming into the house that father tried to talk to me and I just said get out of my face going to my room embarrassed. Knowing that was my only happiness I just stayed in my room for a while that turned in to couple of days. Then later in the week coming home from work I got a call and it was Sosha as we talked and she said she loves me its ok and I cried a little telling her I love her too sorry. That made my day and rest of the week much better but then she had some sad news her parents somehow found out I was 21yrs old not 18yrs old because their neighbor knew someone at my job told them my age so I couldn't come up there to see her anymore and now put her in trouble all for us to have precise time what a way to lose a sweet girlfriend.

16

WANTS OUT
OF REACH

Headed home upset came into house as my parents asking me where I had been. Just told them that her parents said to me not to see their daughter anymore because of my age as my parents were so happy especially that father because he didn't want me to have a normal happiness anyway. So, I just went to my room all depressed for a while. That last week of April it was a Thursday and I was home from work in my room then got a call from Sosha and was surprised to hear from her as she was upset. I apologized to her and said we would find a way to sneak and see each other still and I just thank God he still was helping me still hold on to something joyful.

At home there was nothing to do on weekends, time passed on and Sosha had went to her prom without me but I didn't let it bother me. That father was still bothering me about my stomach problems but I tried to keep away from him in every way.

Still wanting to talk to Sosha with her about to graduate and I wanted to see where we were with the relationship. So, went outside and called from a payphone and she picked up I said hi and she told me she missed me and loved me but also said she going to college in September and that she didn't want to break up with me. I was happy that God has made sure that the happiness in my life with Sosha still was intact.

The next few weeks Sosha and I snuck around as we had lunch at my job and talked with her telling me her parents aren't mad at me anymore about my age but don't want me seeing her anymore. So, we didn't let that stop us and still enjoyed time together and would set up our couple more times.

She asked me if we could try to be intimate again and I agreed as we kissed and hugged and she went home while me smiling knowing God still was in control.

The next day I got ready to see Sosha and came prepared for our special day at her house. So, I left the house prepared with gifts and made it to her house. Rang the doorbell once as she opened the door and it quickly closed, we slowly went upstairs to her room as she looked nice. Then I still was nervous taking my clothes off as she went into the bathroom, I was talking to God please make this nice. Sosha came out with rob on then we started kissing as she was on top of me as I slowly put the gifts on and then we finally had consummated our love. It also happened to be my birthday month July too so it was the best one ever as we just sat there together like we were in space speechless. So, she told me I must hurry up and leave before her parents get home and I kissed her saying love her and she said it back as I was skipping singing all way home a happy boy. Summer continued and was going well with me working and that father not touching me too plus had a loving caring girlfriend in Sosha what else could I thank God for. So, me and Jevone was escaping a lot outside during the week play basketball and would run into all the guys of the neighborhood talking trash. Until one guy Rich said something about Sosha and I ask him to repeat it so he said Sosha been with Timothy guy that likes to run a lot. I just lost it and went after Rich throwing the basketball at him saying your lying as Jevone got me off him said let's go and he calmed me down said he could be lying but we will find out okay as I was in a mad daze couldn't wait to talk to Sosha let her know what people are saying about her is not true.

The next day I told Jevone I was going to confront Sosha about it so we waited until the afternoon on a Saturday and told our parents we going outside to play but instead went rite to Sosha house as Jevone waited at the bench. I rung doorbell and it was her mother as I said hello is Sosha there and she said sure come on in so she said hi and I ask could we talk about something in private and we went into the basement. I looked her in her eyes ready to cry as I said somebody said you was with Timothy together in this house did something happened. Then Sosha started to cry saying yes it just happened by accident I am so, so sorry and I lost it said your nasty and was disgusted told her you never loved me but cheated on me with Timothy. I ran up the stairs she tried to grab my arm saying she loves me but I didn't want to hear it just left out her house angry heading home to Jevone telling him what happened and wanting to find out where Timothy lived to go there and beat him up. The next day Sunday I found out where Timothy lived so me and Jevone went to his house later and bang on the door as he opened it saying what's up and I said you need to come outside so we can talk but he knew it wasn't anything good so he didn't and I just came out said loud we going to get you and that's when he closed the door. It felt good letting it out as we went home to sleep thru night.

I went home that night angry and upset and slept that way into Sunday afternoon did nothing that day. Just stayed in my room and then went back to work for the rest of the week. I thought about calling Sosha and hadn't talked to her in two months but was still too disgusted and mad to talk to her.

Later found out that one of our friends was having a house party in the neighborhood so Jevone and I decided to go even though I found out that Sosha was going to be there. I wasn't sure how to feel seeing her there after the cheating. So as week ended that day was here for the party and still wanting to go with Jevone, I started not to be that angry. Said what's up to cool people and then saw Sosha there with her girlfriend but didn't see Timothy there knowing I hurt him. When a slow song came on it hit me and I just went to Sosha asked her to dance. We danced and kissed then went for a walk outside talking as she said she was sorry. I asked her if she wanted to be together again and she said yes but told me she was going away to college January 12th. I really wanted to make our relationship work so we just enjoyed our weekend together she left.

With the week here and still had a nice one with Sosha a temp agency called and said I had an interview for another job. In the meantime, my parents were getting ready to move soon so we were again on the run.

That Monday came and I was excited about the interview for a position of Data Entry. The time of year was making me happier too because it was Christmas and I had Sosha back so it was a lot to celebrate though my family still was.

> On Christmas I did something bold and called Sosha's house and her that father answered. I wished them Merry Christmas and a Happy New Year he said thank you and asked did I want to speak to Sosha. I said yes and we talked and then met at the park, hugging and kissing. It was then time to go and I told her once more that I was so happy we were back together.

A busy work week ended and then we received a letter from Terance saying he is coming home. He was out of the service and while I was happy to see him still was afraid that he and that father would fight.

17

A PAINFUL FREE DETOUR

The next day I went to find out about the new job of Data Entry inputting insurance claims so I needed to pay attention to do it right. After that, I went to work giving my two weeks notice. My coworkers were happy for me but said they were sad to see me go and that was a great feeling not from family so once work was over, I called Sosha and we met up.

We met at our normal spot park bench and it was cold out but it didn't feel too bad. We talked about her going off to school. I already missed her just thinking about it. I told her I loved her and then we kissed at the park knowing this will be the last time I see her and didn't want to go as she cried and I did also.

Later we both went home as I headed in the house to bed and cried myself to sleep. The next day I arrived at work got there met the boss and they immediately put me to work. The process was slow paced and I was careful not to make mistakes. I was looking forward to seeing Terance that night but had to focus on work.

The next couple of days at work were filled with note taking and I finished out the week well.

Week was good but then we had Terance coming home with his Fiancee' but not sure how my parents would react toward him.

So that day came Saturday Terance rang the doorbell and mom opened the door hugging Terance and said hi to his Fiancee' Julie as we were nice to her that father still wanted to argue with him as I was just ready for it to be over. He wanted to argue about how he left us in front of his Fiancee' who we hadn't met.

Finally, it was time for Terance and his Fiancee' to go so we said bye but not that father still angry and embarrassing us.

The next month, April went well and I was doing a fantastic job at work. I just kept to myself and worked and came home and things are going all right. However, the peace didn't last with that father came in one day and yelled at Terance because he was living at our house without a job.

So, we had to get Terance away from that father to cool off in our bedroom before they fight. Later I heard the door open and closed meaning Terance left as I hoped he went on a walk to cool down. I stayed up rest of the day and night waiting for him come back because I didn't want our parents to let him in and there to be more arguing. Almost falling asleep the doorbell rang and I ran down there to open the door it was Terance as he came in didn't say anything but I told him just keep trying to get a job and we both went to bed.

I was still working happily as we had to do more claim applications, 40 a day, so it was a busy couple of months. My parents were saying that Terance could work at that father job at the Bakers Factory. Though that father was sick of Terance in the house he did follow thru setting up a interview for him and that calmed them both from arguing at each other as I was trying to focus on getting my driver license.

Later that week Terance had an interview and then waited to find out if he got it or not as all of us in the family hope he got it so he can be busy working instead at home getting on that father nerves.

With my birthday rolling around nothing special I was turning 21 with nothing or no one to spend it with as Sosha left for college so I just chilled at home with Jevone, Terance saying happy birthday with mom later coming home saying it too except that father was in his bad mood but still enjoyed my day with no abuse towards me thank God. During that week as I came home from work there was a lot of yelling going on with that father angry at Terance because he pulled strings to get him a interview but he didn't want the job and turned it down. That started a huge fight that even made mother mad and they both wanted him out of our house again for not having a job. With all that was coming at Terance he decided to just leave and this time not come back as he told me that I better follow him too but I couldn't as he planned to leave soon. So thru that week I continued trying to stay out more and not come home from work it made my week better. As the week ended, I talked to Terance and he said Sunday he would be leaving as I was sad to hear but happy that he still is escaping this family prison hoping he keep in touch. Knowing he was leaving Jevone, Terance and me went out to play together one last time and hang outside with friends was subtle way to leave us. Thru the weekend was quiet and Sunday was here as Terance was packed ready to leave as mother hugged him crying as me and Jevone shook his hand and little brother and sister wave bye but that father was happy to see him go. All I saw was an older brother that wasn't afraid to start a life without this family.

Though that part of life was sad, work was going well with the temp agency said I was doing well and the company gave me more work. The next couple of days I just stayed focused thru end of the week came and while the manager said I worked well, they hit me with some sad news that they were hiring someone who had more experience. I did my best to smile and keep my cool, not wanting them to know how upset I was knowing it's not fair that things can't go my way at all. So, headed home Upset tired of the let downs and stayed hidden in my room for a while.

After that I tried to look for more work but things were slow and few people were hiring.

December came and I started to get out of my funk just kept filling out more applications with Christmas only three weeks away I saw an ad in the paper for a job at the Fraiction Store and it was for a Copy Position. Immediately I went down to the store and picked up an application to fill out.

As I was sitting there then I was distracted by a nice, young woman walking by and I started to smile for the first time and said hi to her as she said hi back then left on the elevator but I had to concentrate on the application. After turning the application in I decided to walk around the mall and see the nice stores and was happy to spend more time down there.

Then 2 weeks went fast as Christmas and New Year's Eve came and went with nothing to celebrate as I was still upset that I did not have a job and Sosha had slipped away from me to go to college too. As the old year left the same things on my family, same issues just a new year beginning 1990 but still nothing had changed. I was unemployed still and getting frustrated when a phone call came from the company Fraiction Store that I had filled out an application for the Copy Stack position last December. They wanted me to come in for an interview. I told my family about the interview mother and siblings were happy except that father because I wouldn't be around for him to abuse or attack me.

The next day I woke up early, at 6:30am got my clothes together and got out house to catch that trolley to downtown happy positive person on my way to the interview. I met the Supervisor Tracey and she took me to her office telling me about the position and that I would be typing the Matrix Signs into this new system for all 25 stores and would print them out on cardstock as she went through the entire step-by-step process.

They were looking for someone with good typing skills and who was very dependable and able to lift over 50lbs. She looked over my resume and seemed to like it. She said they had a few other people to interview but would let me know as soon as possible. As I left out thanking the manager and hoping they hire me too and not another disappointing year stayed downtown just walking around. But later days went by and I started getting nervous thinking they don't want me and not sleeping well.

By Wednesday a call came in and it was the Fraiction Store

Office saying they wanted to offer me the job. I was so excited and happy God still did for me that mother and the siblings were happy for me also. So, with mother wanting me to look nice she gave me little money to go buy a nice pair of pants and dress shirt downtown and went out happy and hoping this will be my final permanent job.

With my first day here set the alarm for suitable time to get dress and made it downtown okay arriving at work at 8:40am on the elevator and then headed up the floor. I waited for the receptionist and then out came Tracey as she said hi and introduced me to everyone else there.

It was a delightful place and they were showing me how to go in the system and type in the numbers, prices and how to word for advertisements on signs as the day went by fast.

Leaving to go home I said goodnight and went on the elevator with all these girls. I was a little nervous but smiled on the inside as I made it through that day loving the workplace and found it to be a creative company.

That first week my boss Tracey said I did excellent job and now comes the test as they had me completing five requisitions. Taking took good notes before so I referred to them and was meeting my coworkers as I talked to guy named Alfonso and it felt comfortable in the workplace.

Enjoying a nice weekend going over my notes not too much but just enough I was ready for the work week ahead. The more I worked the more people I met and really was liking the environment. With me finishing that week without making any mistakes for my second week was a happy feeling. And did well for two months straight getting paid used it to buy a few more items of clothing. Since I worked in the Fraiction Store employees was given a 15% discount on items at the Fraiction Store and The Fraiction Stores. So, using the discount was a great as I started going a lot to lunch with the Alfonso and he introduced me to Sufon and Lanley. We talked about sports and other things and I was happy to have real guy friends. Outside was getting nice May was here and I was happy because I kept meeting new people at work. Getting to know the guys more; Sufon had a wife and kids two boys and Lanley had a wife and daughter while Alfonso was single. Telling them I had three brothers and one sister happy seeing that I never had nice people to open to but did and knew it was okay.

At home things was still same mean that father and mother arguing about silly stuff but my parents told me that my mother's grandmother was sick. Later that father pulled all of us aside said that mother was terribly upset and needed our support.

We made plans next weekend to go see grandmother that would be nice for us to get out of that house. I was still staying happy about my new job and staying outside of the house every chance I could. Later that weekend we headed to see grandmother and she was happy to see us but looking still sick as mother cried like knowing her health is getting worse but we were glad to get out see our cousins too. Heading home with us seeing grandmother made my family real quiet where nobody was arguing just worried about mother losing grandmother. As weeks were quiet one mother decided that she didn't like the house anymore and told that father she wants to move as it wasn't a suitable time to be doing this with grandmother not well. But this is how my family is trying to escape paying bills so again we were running with no plan at all.

18

PUSHING
LEAVE WAY

With all this mess going on in my family I tried to stay focus on my new job as we were to move quickly and had to tell my substitute boss that I would be moving to New Jersey at end of this week and he told me to go to the human resources department to fill out paperwork.

That Friday my boss was back but she had something to tell us that she will be leaving us for parental leave and we were happy for her as she told us we will have a substitute supervisor from Art and Design Department Mr. Dren covering our department until she is replaced so we wished her good luck and finished working through the rest of the day. I left going home was tired but now had to help get us ready to sneak out of this Philly house to move to New Jersey in the middle of the night. I got home that Friday night and my family was waiting for me to get in and help boxed things up as that father went to get the Handler truck later into the night. So, we finished packing as quick as posble and into trash bags too while everybody in neighborhood was sleeping was our sneak out time. With that father bad back he had to drive so we took a route toward 1-95 South downtown to the Bannon Francis bridge and drove another

45 minutes. It took us almost 1 ½ hours to get there with that father driving slow too and never been to this part of New Jersey was a new experience for all of us. As it was pitch dark out but finally made it to this big house with a long big front grass and a garage too looking like a single home that again we couldn't afford. With mother and my little sister and brother going into the house with what we had in truck it was still time for me and Jevone and that father go back to house get the rest of all the furniture so our night was just beginning. Getting back to house me and Jevone had to be that father's eyes driving back so late at night as we made it back to the Philly house and spent two hours loading as much furniture as we could back to New Jersey house. Heading back to the new house still took us another hour just to unload and then made one last trip back to old house throwing whatever into the Handler truck in no type of neat way as me and Jevone was dead tired. We finally got to the new place and just unloaded throwing stuff into the living room and basement finishing finally at 2am in the morning then just locked the Handler up as we all just slept on the floor didn't even care.

The next day I woke up to my parents cooking breakfast in the new house kitchen all happy like we really living in a fantasy house that I know we won't be here long either but all I was trying to figure out how am I going to get to my job and not lose it from New Jersey. So, me and Jevone look up the bus schedule and for mother to go to work too or that father will drive her but still it was no care in the world for how we were to get to work. Later we got the furniture and bags together then putting the beds and stuff into the living room and out of the garage. I spent the next two days trying to know where to walk to catch the New Jersey Traveler bus to Philly for work was a couple of blocks walk.

I just slept thru the weekend as Monday was here as me and Jevone had to walk 10 blocks just to catch our buses as mine came at 7:30 am bus but Jevone had to leave later then me but knew he had to get his walk on too. It was a long commute and by the time I got work it felt like it was a 2hr ride but made it there barely not late ready to work and hoping I get this down better to be on time and needed to get my rest.

This continued for weeks until I got so tired of catching the bus that I tried not just once but 3 times trying to get my license and succeed with happiness about that.

The months went by quickly and it was now Christmas time as I worked overtime a lot just to have my own money plus giving my parents money too.

Don't know why that father helped with the decorating with him being the one for all this abuse and pain in this family.

In meantime Jevone had a girlfriend and I was jealous about that because he was out of this house a lot and not being attacked.

Though Christmas around the corner there was still the issue of our sick grandmother at this time of the year with our together time was only for her.

That weekend, mother was still concerned about grandmother and we finally heard from Terance on that Christmas Day wishing us a Merry Christmas and informed us that he was okay and staying with a woman. So that was one happy time but also peace of mind too.

The next week was last week of this year 1990 towards New Year's Eve working but got in trouble for being late again for work and had to stay late because of it but it was okay I needed the money anyway.

Made it home with my parents there Kevin, Bernadette on couch as we were watching TV but I took a nap and later woke up as my siblings was downstairs counting down the New Year 1991 and it happened as I just said Thank You Jesus getting my siblings and me thru another year and went rite back to bed. The weekend me and Jevone took that father car and took my first time driving the car heading to the store to get food and happy to be driving.

On Monday Mr. Dren said that Candice is going to another department as we said we miss her as he said in two weeks we will have somebody coming in to replace her and that he wants me to be a substitute supervisor of the department as it shocked me that he asked me instead of Alfonso who been her all this time but I accepted and was so happy but hoping my coworkers still work with me too.

At home mother said that grandmother was not getting any better so she wanted to really see grandmother but then my parents started to argue as usual I just went to my room, got on my knees, and prayed for peace within the family.

The next day I went to work ready to do my substitute supervisor duties and as I was waiting for the elevator then I saw that young beautiful woman again and went to her a little nervous and shy just said hi. She said hi back then somehow, I told her my name is Daire and asked for her name and she said its Kim Butter as I said okay bye going up on the elevator smiling for a while. Later taking a break I then ask Candice do she know this young woman name Kim Butter and she said ok she use to work here. As I kept smiling told Candice that I like her she told me to talk more to her next time and I will.

As the week finished great at home Mother and that father went to see sick grandmother and they stayed not long but saying upset a lot with grandmother couldn't even talk. I immediately went to my room and ask Jesus for his help.

At work I was ready to talk to the new girl. One day waiting for the elevator to go back to work from lunch when I saw Kim Butter and I introduced myself and we talked as I said have a good day heading back to work with a smile thru the entire day. Working here was so great for me but then another coworker Alfonso decided he was tired of this place and gave his two weeks notice so I wished him well knowing I have no reason to complain. As I got home mother was still upset about grandmother and all we could do was try to not upset her anymore but with this family that been years of problems for us. With me still happy working it was then time for Alfonso to say goodbye to all of us and we wished him the best. Later that day I was able to talk to Candice in the hallway outside her new job about setting something up to meet Kim Butter that she could talk to her.

While at home mother wasn't doing well and she had a feeling that grandmother passed away and just as she told us that she received a phone call and it was true, she had. We all hugged, comforting mother the best we could.

Later mother with her sister had to discuss funeral arrangements together and bring the family all together was something new to mother since not really talking to them much. Thru the following week we all did our best to help at home for mother. Though it was sad, I knew God was still in control and had told my boss and coworkers that my grandmother passed and had to go to the funeral in two weeks. They were supportive and understood. Work was busy with us short staff not having another coworker so I was doing extra work and coming home tired going rite to sleep. Then it was that day came of grandmother funeral as we all got dress heading up there in Philadelphia as we saw relatives we didn't know or had not seen in a long time it was a tearful awakening as we all said our last goodbyes to grandmother. There was an open casket and no eye was dry that day as we went to the cemetery and buried her. Afterwards we went to her home to celebrate her life and all prayed together saying now is the time for loving each other while we are alive and she was now watching us. After hugging and kissing everybody we went home mother was in her room the rest of the weekend.

With the funeral tough on my mother still my job was going well and still working my body off as a temporary supervisor too when I came home my parents gave me some peace and quiet. Being 22yrs old still single in a family just hoping Kim Butter would find me interesting.

I was happy and tired from work. Jevone invited his girlfriend Jeanine over to meet us all I thought was suicide but she was nice what I thought but my parents was still but still not staying long Jevone and Jeanine, his girlfriend, got ready to go and left.

The next day at work I had to get ready for the new employee his name was Rocco and we introduced ourselves as we showed him around. He was a quick learner and by the end of the first week he had done well. I told the boss he was on time copying everything as Mr. Dren smiled and said it was nice that we are all working as a team and we continued that rhythm finishing months ahead of schedule. I never thought to see myself as a leader and others appreciate me so much that it was a great feeling.

With Jevone spending a lot of time with Melissa my parents

were getting upset saying he is changing like her family and that is a remarkable thing to see my brother happy outside of this family and hope and pray that for me too. As summer passed, I was taking a break coming back to work to elevators and ran into Kim Butter at the bench so I said hi and she said hi back. I asked if she were okay and invited her to lunch one day as she said maybe and that she would get back to me and that was the best day I ever had that help me see there is something good in me she will see.

Later getting home all the sudden old things started to happen again with that father talking about he does miss me a lot and stuff as I did my best to stay away from him praying God please continue to protect me from him so I can finally one day escape from his abuse as I headed up to my safe room cave.

Though I was making good money, my parents took every penny. It upset off me and Jevone giving them both $100 and kept the rest to save for our own apartments to escape this nonsense one day. With November came and I began looking for an apartment to rent was also spending a lot of time after work with my coworkers not trying to rush home either. My parents did not like it but I did not care what they thought and still had plans to ask Kim Butter out too.

During the next few weeks mothers became upset because she missed her mother since it was around the holidays and it was still hurting her as we did our best to really help keep mother better by showing some type of peace within us as a family.

I did my best to ignore that father as well even though he would try to talk to me in the house because God has shut his attacks down on me and he is in control. So, as I was happy going to work one day then I ran into Candice in the hallway as she told me she was having a party for her birthday and she had invited Kim Butter, me, and other coworkers. I was so, so happy to be invited to anything as that was all I needed to keep staying happy plus to get to see Kim Butter there too and have my chance to be bold and ask her out God is Good.

19

WALKING HEART STRONG

That Friday at home I thought about not wanting to go to the party alone so I asked if Jevone could come along with me please as he said okay just this one time and I said thanks as we of course had to ask that father to borrow the car and that was a pain to go thru asking us all these questions plus mother getting mad saying yall better not be trying to have precise time and stuff just too much. So, after all that mess we still got it together on how to get up to the party that was in north Madin street. That Saturday we just chilled, ate some cereal then later we got ready for the party and never been up there before so it took us one hour to get there but made it and saw Candice said, "Happy Birthday" and introduced Jevone to her and then I saw Kim Butter. I just said hi to her and she said hi back as me and Jevone walked around the party enjoying ourselves and then later got it together and finally asked Kim Butter to dance and she said yes and it lite up my heart that I could already tell she was the one I had been waiting for.

We had a wonderful time dancing off two songs and then she heard her favorite song come on and said can we dance one more time and I said of course and it was so great that I could not stop smiling. It was exciting time with her as we left dance floor and I got her some soda to drink for her and myself and just came out saying can I get your phone number and she said yes giving it to me with a smile back. As the party was over Jevone was dancing too and had a fun time, we had to get back to the prison house because we told our messy parents we be back by 1am and it was already 12:30am so leaving was a priority. Me and Jevone was talking all the way home in that father car as he saw me dancing with Kim Butter and then I told him I got her number we were slapping each other high five it was great night. Still made it home but of course that father was up rite at the door when we came in saying what took us so long as we said it is 1am but that father tried to lie saying yall supposed to be here 1230am so we kept our happiness going upstairs smiling. So, what a great weekend that I sneak on the house phone to call Kim Butter just to say hi and we talked but short because my parents were watching me and tried to listen in on the phone conversations too. I eventually had to go outside to a pay phone or at my job and call her too. Over the next few months we talked a lot hoping to know each other but he not to know my family. She was one that took things slowly as we talked but for me still turned quickly into strong feelings for her and was not sure if she will receive it from me or not but prayed that she would.

When I got home opened the door to find mother crying because Jevone said he was going to move in with Melissa his girlfriend in apartment. He said sorry but my parents would not listen to him at all as I then started to get mad with Jevone begging my brother to please, please do not leave me with that father by myself. But Jevone said he cannot stay here anymore with them as he told us he is leaving us this weekend and this is his last time here. Then that father was yelling saying you are wrong leaving us and upsetting your mother currently when she still hurting from loss of her mother too. But Jevone still said he sorry he loves us but must be on his own and have happiness and then it was hitting me that I started to get scared again thinking about all the abuse by that father again and now no one not even Jevone will be here to help me. So, thru the night and weeks I just did not talk to him for leaving me now as he saw my anger these last days with him. As that Sunday came where Jevone packed up and had Melissa his girlfriend coming to pick him up he came to mother as she could not hug him but still hugged Kevin and Bernadette, that father just looked at him and then I just said you wrong for leaving me as he got his things together for the last time seeing him with his girlfriend outside leaving me behind to be abused with no one else to help me.

As that first week went by coming home, I was not in any rush to hurry home to be attacked and abused again with Jevone leaving me by myself that I took my time coming home not until 8pm to be left alone from that father. Then over the next few weeks Jevone tried to call the house to just talk but our parents were very disrespectful to him yelling and even cussing at him so he did not call for a while.

With me scared to go home it still was a better summer as I finding some type of happiness establishing a good relationship talking with Kim Butter and thanked God that she was in my life with the pain I kept inside of my family. After work I would go to a payphone talk to her said how and we had a friendly conversation that she told me of her new job working at Armor Cross. I was happy for her and then one day asked to meet her one day so she said yes and we set that up for a Friday night.

Mean time still was trying to adjust to Jevone being gone these past months it was extremely hard to sleep at night keeping my eyes open just wanting to run outside and not look back. Heading to work I had plans to meet Kim Butter for lunch at Highten street was a great feeling. So, caught the trolley and saw her as I came up the steps outside her job looking so, so beautiful as we got together talking with me staring how nice and pretty she looked in her dress. At lunch I talked to her about my brother Jevone moving out leaving me by myself and she was like I understand as she told me she been on her own since she 16. At that moment I had so much respect for her and said I got to get back to work but said it was great to see you as she said bye and I jumped on the trolley back to work with a smile of peace. Returning to work everyone could tell I was in a happy mood and then asked God to keep Kim Butter in my life of what joy that I never had before. Still the past couple of weeks it was getting so tired of coming home late to this house with mother and that abusive that father ready to attack me and start that abuse again on me. So, heading home on the New Jersey bus it started to get to me on that I did not want to be here anymore by myself so I took a leap of faith hearing God and decided to escape and get out of here. Once I decided came in the house straight to my room and was getting anything of my stuff together in my book bag as mother came in my room asking what am I doing and just said leaving cannot stay her. Mother started crying saying now you too trying to break your mother's heart and why me and Jevone want to hurt her. Then that father came in yelling saying you cannot leave you got nowhere to go and I said yes I do now leave me alone or I start talking the real reason I leaving so he backed off. As my little sister Bernadette and Kevin looking on crying too said I need my own space away from yall be my own man. Mother asked where am I going and just said anywhere but staying here maybe a friend place but not knowing who still gathered my stuff hugging little brother and sister looked at that father and tried to hug mother as she cried and told them love yall walking out not looking back. So scared but feeling little okay walking to catch the Philadelphia bus ride the only person God told me to call was Kim Butter so I got on the bus and hoping at this late time of the night after 9pm she be home to help me. Finally got down there and went rite to a pay phone praying she notice the Friday night and she did. I said hi and she asked who is this I said its Daire is this a tough time and Kim Butter said she is with her girlfriend and I paused then ask could I come over to see you and she said okay as I took her address down and headed out. So, took the trolley from downtown to get there was 30 minutes and got off at twenty street then started walking to her street with my two bags and finally found her apartment of 3 stories but had no idea what floor she was on. Just started to yell her name out three times and she came to the window looked down and I said sorry it is me Daire and told me she be right down go front door so I waited.

As I stood at the door nervous then she opened the door and said hi seeing my two book bags I just came out said are you busy as he explained her girlfriend but you still can come in. I went up these long steps with my two book bags up to the third floor to her nice one room apartment with a kitchen, living room, and bedroom. I said sorry for asking to come over so late telling her that my family is controlling and could not take it anymore needed to get out but do not have a place to go. Then asked her if I could stay with her for a few weeks and would help her pay rent until I find my own place. She looked at me with two bags for a few minutes as I was praying that she gave me a chance, then said she think about it and it is late. Had told me I can sleep on the couch that night thanked her and thanking God he still helping me.

The next day Saturday I woke up thought it was a dream then looked around and know it was not as I said good morning to Kim Butter and asked if I could stay here as she said yes then went thanking God but needed to use her bathroom to clean up. I told her I respected her independence and wished I could have done that a long time ago. Later said Jevone and I were tired of the abuse from our parents for years but still left out some of the details.

As time passed, Kim Butter told me she had to go to the grocery store and I said can we go together I have some money so we went for a long walk but it was enjoyable day and helped her shop and carry the grocery home as we talked a little then came home putting food away relaxed, listening to music and I was so quiet but happy she let me stay here as I fell asleep to the great peaceful music. The next day, Sunday, we woke up and had a good morning talking more just listening to the radio and then told me she wanted to go to church but had not found a church to go so far. So, we talked some more and enjoyed our evening together with me not Upset or being attacked just a happy peaceful time with a great friend in Kim Butter.

The next day I woke up at 7 am as she did also and she told me we could catch the trolley together. I thought that was nice as we took turns using the bathroom to get dressed then an hour later it was time to go. She locked the door as we went down the steps and out the door to catch the trolley. We sat together as she looked nice in her dress and I could not believe any of this was happening. I was so happy just kept thanking God all the way to work.

As she got off at ninety street I said have a good day and she said bye then stayed on the trolley to work with fullness of joy that I could never have imagined. At work Malandy notice how happy I was and glad to see it from me into the rest of the day was not depressed and did not even think about calling my parents. As the day ended, I left out headed to Kim Butter apartment and once there she opened the door let me in and she asked me how was my day and I said great then ask her the same she said good. We relaxed and then later she had cooked spaghetti for dinner and it was great as we continued to have an enjoyable time together that I never want to leave.

After dinner we talked more about her family and little of mines and I wanted it that way as she understood and as we continued talking about her two sisters and brother on how happy they stuck together even when she got her own place at early age was nice to hear for a change. Then it was time to head to sleep still had work tomorrow as she slept in her bed while I was on the couch with music on to help us sleep better too. The next day I woke up so happy wanted to do something for her so got up early to ask her if I could iron her clothes to show my appreciation. She said sure while she was making some eggs and it was great too with me drinking hot tea and she had coffee then later we got dress for work and left out together to catch the trolley to downtown.

At work I was having a wonderful day all because of Kim Butter so I called her at work see how her day was going and she said hi I fine. Then I let her know I am finally going to call my parents to let them know how I am doing as Kim Butter was a little worried.

Heading to her apartment knowing I got to get this done at Kim Butter apartment after work and not be ashamed. Later I asked to call my parents once on her house phone and she said sure. So, after dinner I decided to call and it was my mother picked up the phone saying who is this and I said it is me Daire as she started yelling at me said your wrong arguing and then leaving us. I was about to yell back at her but Kim Butter told me to hang up the phone so I did.

Knowing how silly my family was acting had no choice but to leave them alone rite now and get thru that night while we were sleeping knowing my parents will never change. Later that night her phone rang waking Kim Butter up as she answered it as it was my mom calling all late asking to speak to me. So, Kim Butter upset woke me up gave me the phone and told my mother its late as she asked what yall doing playing around and I just hung up. Knowing this was not good for me trying to live here with Kim Butter and earn her respect is the hurt my family does as we tried to get some rest.

The next day, Wednesday we woke up and Kim Butter was not happy and had good reason too. She was upset and did not say anything to me as we still headed out to work together and knowing she would never understand why I still love them despite what they have done to me.

So, as I got to work still bit worried if I still had a place to stay then decided to do something about it and call my parents before I started work. As I dialed the number that father picked up asking who is this and I said it is me Daire at payphone and he started to say he missed me and I can come back anytime. But instead, I threaten that father saying if you do not stop mother from calling Kim Butter's apartment then I will tell her all the abusing you done to me from age 13yrs old to 19yrs old. So next thing happened he said okay, okay and I hung up trying to hurry up get to work on time. Still upset tried my best to not let my coworkers know it finished work somehow in okay way. Time then to go home heading to hopefully still a place to stay I was scared to think what Kim Butter felt about my family and me. Then got there rang the bell three times before she finally opened the door and knowing she was still mad at me I quickly apologized again to her. Kim Butter said also I need to talk to them, straighten them out, and tell them stop calling this apartment or she will call them back telling them off herself.

The next day at work I was numb and upset about everything going on in my life. During my lunch break I tried to call my parents again at the office whispering telling them to again please do not call Kim Butter apartment again and hopefully they take me seriously as well.

Later going home, I did not know what to do or say to Kim Butter to make things any better as I got to the apartment and she had an upset face on her stating your parents calling again!! Then still being quiet we got into arguing more and she had enough that I was told this is your last week here I need to leave by the weekend. So just taking it in hurting way I could not hold in the tears and was crying from ear to ear non-stop but it did not faze Kim Butter she was tired as I could not sleep knowing I heading back to the prison where all my pain was at.

As Saturday came, I was still so upset that why cannot God help me escape from this abuse as I called my parents mother answered and told her can that father pick me up for stay with yall as she broke out in happiness saying she missed me on the phone wanting me to come home and I just said fine. She burst into happiness then got that father on phone as he said I glad you coming back but couldn't stand his voice just said be her by 11am and hung up. I could think of was that there is now no more happiness for me heading back there with that father as I was getting my two bags together while Kim Butter didn't even care and that father was here in no time so I said sorry and bye to Kim Butter but still no response as she followed me to the door. That father was there with the car door open while I was ready to start crying again but what good will it do so, just quickly got in the car said nothing to that father smiling saying miss you, while Kim Butter didn't even say goodbye but quickly closed her door. All I could feel was anger wanting to punch that father rite in face and cuss him out as they have again ruined my happiness. Heading home all I did was the silent treatment in the car and didn't even look that father as he was smiling like he got me back again. We got back home and my mother opened the door hugging me like she hadn't seen me in year yet still I didn't hug back was so, so angry just said I tired need to rest closing and locking my bed room door feeling like why God do this to me again as I laid in the bed with one eye open eventually cried myself to sleep.

That Monday morning, I got up and threw some clothes on and didn't care about anything still Upset that I had defended this family for nothing to be stuck back in the cave of abuse. Still thinking about Kim Butter upset my parents hurt my chance of getting to know her but praying God gives me another chance for us. So still getting up early out of this house going to work catching the New Jersey bus just wanting to stay away from that prison house even after work not in no hurry to go home. As I continued coming home late from work and not running into no abusive that father or mother still got thru those two weeks with God on my side. Then on a Wednesday my parents wanted to talk to me as I got in the house still praying mother said they been talking to Terance worried about him having a place to live and inviting him to come home but in the mean time I didn't care because this place is and don't want to be here.

So, the weeks went by and I still went to work and came home straight to my room but this time my parents had something to tell me. That father and mother opened my bedroom door and said they have some news to tell me that they still had the Silvers Place house in Philadelphia. And Terance has been staying there for the past 2 weeks but nobody was to know and that father needs me to move in with him to keep an eye on Terance because they still don't trust him that he might have somebody in there where nobody not to be. So, they ask me if I want to stay with him only to keep eye on him too as I said let me think about it heading to bed praying God will make this better for me. Later waking up that Saturday went to my parents and said I would be okay going over to the old house in Philadelphia to stay with Terance. So, my parents made plans for me to go over there Sunday and all I could say still thanking God for blessing me with another way of escape from my abusive that father.

It was Sunday morning and I had to get my stuff together to move with Terance so mother made me breakfast saying she will miss me as I hugged her, Bernadette, and Kevin but nothing towards that father. We had to leave early while on the block some people where at church and others still sleep was suitable time to go down there. So, we left out and that father driving me I didn't want to hear nothing he had to say though he tried to say he loves me but that's been a lie for years. It didn't take long get there and that father knocked on the door as Terance opened the door and I just said hey what's up brother as we shook hands and that father check the place just in case, he had somebody here. As that father left and I got my stuff out car and he said to both of us keep the place clean and be quiet then left. Then Terance said it gets dark but because no electricity so we have flashlight and sleep in your clothes because it gets cold and use your book bag as a pillow. As we ate dinner, he started talking about how our parents were still the same abusive parents and I agreed but we also talked about girls and how many Terance been with was good to see we still brothers after it all. Then we went to sleep on the floor for our first brother with brother time together hoping this will be a start of real new chance for me too.

The next day I woke up as it was late but was happy to not be at that cave in New Jersey with my parents so got dress quick but happy said see you later Terance on my way heading to work with a safe smile.

When I got there is had a great big smile good morning to everybody and thru the day towards lunch too was the best feeling I had in years. Still had to call that father to tell him that yesterday everything was okay with Terance and then asked if he could bring by the rest of my clothes since I be staying with him longer. Then that father had to add something to the end stating that I owe him for this and all I could do was hang up on him knowing I am at work don't want to go off here that is what he wants anyway.

Still had a good day at work left exhausted because I hadn't slept well the night before since just moving in with Terance but on way home, I started to think about Kim Butter. Since I still had her phone number just not sure if I should call her or she even talk to me.

The weekend came and I woke up saw that Terance wasn't awake yet so I went back to sleep for a while but then later the doorbell rung and it was mother at door as I opened it and she quickly came in hug me and Terance with rest of my clothes and then left out with that father in car.

Once they left Terance talked about how he didn't miss our parents again still angry and so was I. Terance later decided to go out for a bit and I was glad to have some time to myself relaxing and listened to music for a while began thinking about calling Kim Butter but was not ready because still felt the embarrassment of them calling her apartment so just went to bed. Next day woke up slept fairly good and ready going to work on time but notice Terance wasn't home so still got ready to head out the doorbell rung and I was thinking it was Terance but it was Jevone and I was shocked what you doing here. Jevone said Terance let him stay here but I still asked why what happened to you and your girlfriend apartment you left us for. He said they couldn't afford it so I just said okay well got to get to work and shook his hand left out still happy going work and heading to work glad Jevone okay now we back together again as the 3 brothers. Work was even better I was getting our projects done as Malandy and Rocco working good too so rest of the day was quiet but smooth. Got home as Jevone and Terance was there and we talked about each having food money. So, I said we need to stick together and help each other out too unlike our parents as we relaxed talked more about sports then headed to bed.

The next day woke up feeling good got dress headed to work in better spirits and made it to office work with Malandy and Rocco we had a lovely day and some laughter thru the day too.

That Friday I got home and Terance and Jevone were talking about getting a TV so we would have something to watch. They asked me for some money since I got paid and said that it cost $50. They had $30 so I gave them $20 and saved the rest of my money for my food. Then we put all our money together to buy food. Over the weekend on Sunday afternoon, we were watching TV and talking about girlfriends. Terance asked me what's up with mine and why don't I call her and see what's up. I decided to tell them both that I don't have one yet just talking to her and Jevone well him and Jeanine are still together just he trying to get it together. So, we talked more but then Terance said why don't you call her and not waist time so I got dress it was after 8pm walked to a pay phone hoping she pick up the phone and let me talk to her take a chance. The phone rung 4 times and I was about to hang up when Kim Butter picked up saying who is this in angry way and I said it's me Daire calling from payphone. She then said what do you want and where are you calling from and told her I in Philly at a corner store payphone. Close to my old parent's house staying there with my two brothers the past month but wanted to see how you was doing. Also told her I was sorry for what happened and hoped it was okay to call and she said will think about it but asked what was wrong with my family are they. Just said sorry I am trying to remove myself from my family but thanked her and appreciated her helping me. She said I could call her again another day and think about things between us as Kim Butter said goodnight and I said goodnight hanging up phone on happy note. So, going to work was better for me and I even had talked to my coworkers about Kim Butter as Malandy and Rocco suggested continue talking to her and hope things work out.

At home Terance asked how my day was and I said okay as he told me Jevone would be home late. So, I ate a sandwich and got dress to go outside on the pay phone to call Kim Butter.

So, she picked up and I said hi how was your day as Kim Butter said okay but then I asked did you think about us still being friends and she said still unsure but wants us to continue talking was good to hear. So, Kim Butter asked me about work and I said okay saying Malandy is funny and she asked hope you like your new job too. We continued to talk for 45 minutes but my fingers started to get numb and I asked could we talk again tomorrow my hands are getting cold and she said okay goodnight and I said goodnight with a happy smile.

I felt so alive again just talking to her made me feel my heartbeat more as coming quickly back in the house Terance was up and he asked me what happened. Me and Terance talked and I said we had friendly conversation and I am starting to like her as he laughed but said good and stop being scared go after her so it was a great night with time to get some sleep.

Another week was here March weather was not as cold but we had still snow as I went to work singing to myself and once the day was over and I left work on time trying to hurry home to get to that payphone call to Kim Butter. We talked awhile about our weekends and our days at work as she talked about her ex- boyfriend that didn't treat her right and I shared that my ex- girlfriend left me for college so we both had a lot to talk about.

I felt more and more that we were getting closer and just finally asked her if we were just friends or more than that and she said she had to think about it as I told her it's time for me to get back in the house its late but have a good night and Kim Butter said goodnight to me as a smile continued my face all the way home thanking God for another good peaceful night sleep.

As work was great then with talking more to Kim Butter was great too and my parents can't reach me or that father attack me feeling good that God is still in control. So, leaving to head quickly home from work saw Jevone said what's up and Terance saying he about to go out too. It hit me Friday wonder what Kim Butter doing so called her and the phone kept ringing so I just waited for her to pick up. Hung up and then called again maybe she cooking or something but still nothing and called back one more time still nothing so I just hung up little upset. Why didn't she tell me yesterday when we talk don't call or she playing me as I started to get mad and went home upset with nothing to say to my brothers just went early to bed. The next few days I hung out with Terance and went shopping for some new clothes as he asked me what happened last night and I just said not good she never answered her phone. So, Terance said and so what call her again don't let that stop you okay if you like her keep going after what you like don't be a punk okay. It felt good for the first time my big brother Terance truly helping me and that's what I needed. So later got back from store while Jevone was relaxing and Terance going to work, I was writing down what I want to say to Kim Butter so I don't leave anything out.

So, with this work week went by fast and it's Friday I still didn't talk to Kim Butter so I decided to not give up like Terance said and went to the corner pay phone called her as it was after 6pm that Friday. I let it ring five times no answer and hung up deciding to just wait 30 minutes she went to store and called her again let it ring this time 6 times but still no answer and frustrated. Finally said that's it decided to go to her apartment and talk to her face to face and see if I fooling myself liking her and find out she like somebody else too would hurt me.

Being its February and still cold out I couldn't let that stop me from going up there to see Kim Butter as I got back to the house and Jevone ask me what's up. I told my brother that she didn't answer the phone but I going up there and he said good find out what's going on. So, got dress quick and left out to catch the trolley not knowing what time the next one comes. As I just made it running to get the trolley sat in my seat starting to get a little nervous not sure what to say to her but then asked God to give me the right words to say in a caring liking her way. With the weather still winter few people on the trolley so it didn't take long to get to her apartment as I got there and took a deep breath then rang her doorbell twice waiting a few minutes. There was no answer so I rang it again and waited but still no answer and things started to come in my head like is she with some guy but calmed down. Still not sure if she is home or out so with the weekend here too know she must come home so I decided to stand out front of her apartment until she comes back. Just hoping Kim Butter still like me and with way we been talking she see I can be a great boyfriend to her but also to ignore my family that I will not let stop me from being happy. With it still cold out I started to walk around for another couple of minutes and all the sudden I saw her walking up toward me. I said hi and she said hi as I told her I was thinking about her and had called a couple of times but didn't get a answer from you so just came up here to see you and Kim Butter said okay. I told her I really liked her and wanted to spend time with her as Kim Butter asked how could we work this out with my family keep bothering us calling and asking us what we doing. So, I told her that I didn't care what they thought anymore and won't let them stop me because I knew you are good for me Kim Butter. I asked her to tell me how she felt and if she didn't feel the same way I would no longer bother her.

She said you don't even know everything about me so how could you like me that quick that is weird and then it hit me that she made fun of me liking her and I said you don't have to be so mean and she said it's because of you family is why and next thing I know we was arguing back and forth for 20 minutes outside in the snow. Finally, I was done and said I leaving be with whoever you want and walk away still hurt how this turned out and let down completely. As Kim Butter went into her apartment didn't say anything to me at all with no like for me because I didn't see it at all tonight. Almost home and then it hit me you know what I going to give her one more piece of my mind so called her from a payphone. As soon as the phone went thru all I could hear was Kim Butter answered crying saying she miss me and never wanted me to leave then I started crying on the phone said sorry I would never leave you again and said I coming back. There was so, so much joy in my heart knowing we was meant to be together running like to hurry get back to the old house ringing the doorbell and Terance let me in with Jevone there and they ask me what happened. I was so excited just said we are happy and she wants me to stay with her at the apartment. They both smiled at me and we shook congratulation handshakes as I got my clothes together for work and to stay with Kim Butter. So, got what I could carry Jevone and Terance said they both happy for me and I left out to go be with my girl catching the trolley back to her place with nothing but smiles from ear to ear on my face. As soon as I got there 40 minutes later, she opened the door and it was automatic we just kissed and I told her sorry and I cared for her so much. She said she cared for me too and we kissed and hugged that night. I told her that I wouldn't let my family stop this promise as Kim Butter understood saying we can make this work and then went to bed holding each other having romantic time and then falling asleep.

The next day we woke up together with smiles of a peaceful night in each other arms as Kim Butter asked me if we were starting a relationship and I told her yes. She then said she happy with me living with her as we both god dress for work feeling so happy together as I am her man feel good.

I went to work so happy with Malandy and Rocco there and told them that Kim Butter were back together. They were happy to hear that as I enjoyed my day and called her for a bit at lunch to say hi and that I miss her already as she said it back to me as I had to get back to work. Once I got back to her apartment after work, we talked about everything and relaxed.

That week went by and I reached out to my brothers see if they okay and they continued say they happy for me and it was great support from them too. I told her just a little of me and myself but she talked more of her was good as she also told me her birthday March 30th is coming up soon and she likes chocolate, balloons, or roses so I had my hands full of choices.

Rest of days were great and we talked more about what we liked and didn't like was so wonderful to do and then waking up next day to her was amazing feeling I could never have imagined thank God. Then I asked her would it be okay for her to meet my brothers and she said yes that be fine so we planned after work to go see them. By taking trolley was a 40 minutes ride then walking from there was 10 minutes and we got there as I ring the doorbell. My brother Terance opened door said hi and then let us in as I introduce Terance and Jevone to Kim Butter as she said hi and they both said she is cut as I smiled. We laughed a little then it was time for us to go so I hugged my brothers and they said bye as we left on our way to continue what God Put Together Let Nothing Separate Us.

We were enjoying our times together and knowing that her family was okay with us being together was all we needed while at work all I was doing smiling from ear to ear with Malandy and Rocco seeing me happy man. Plus, this week was Kim Butter birthday so I had to be ready to give her something or go out and was saving my money well too. The week was great then that special day came it was Kim Butter birthday March 3rd and as she woke up, I was already awake wishing her Happy Birthday hugging her and kissing her as she smiled. Then went to kitchen made her some scrambled eggs for breakfast as she looked at her birthday card that I gave her and smiled with the one balloon too. Kim Butter was all smiles that morning as we both getting dress for work as we started kissing and holding each other almost late for work. I had asked Kim Butter could we go to the movies later as she said yes as we were riding on trolley and before her stop came at ninety street gave her a big birthday kiss as she got off.

As I got to work my coworkers saw me so happy that I told them its Kim Butter birthday today and said I cooked her breakfast and later taking her out to movies as they were happy for me. Then later went to lunch with the fellas Lanley and Sufon as we talked and they ask me are you a happy man and I said yes indeed with such a great feeling what God doing for me and Kim Butter to be together I been thru.

Me and Kim Butter met up together after going to the movies at 40th street and had such a great night enjoying her birthday with me doing the best I could for her as we got home then it hit me, she told me she wants to have precise time and I was in shocked. Still couldn't talk but happy she said go to store and get gifts as I ran to the store quickly knowing that this is our night thanking God for making this possible. Got back as quick as I could while we ate dinner first then had a romantic birthday spending time together time but something came out of my mouth while we were enjoying ourselves that I said Kim Butter I am falling for you and she just smiled as we enjoyed a great night.

The next day Kim Butter still happy enjoying her birthday she later said her lease expires in two months and she been looking for an apartment so I was okay with that helping to find another place for both us to live together. Kim Butter was so good that she had been saving money and has two apartments to look at so I was putting money aside too. Then I started to stay a little overtime to help with the bills too so we would have enough to move at same time. But then it was also time for Kim Butter to let her parents know we are a couple so she called them Thursday night at our apartment after we settled in she called her parents and talk to her mother started telling her she had met a nice guy named Daire and has been see me for 4 months and were now living together then just handed the phone to me out of the moment. I was polite to say hi Mrs. Hoard nice to talk to you and looking forward to meeting you and Mr. Hoard as I gave the phone back to Kim Butter and she then said bye to her nice family. It was a nice night for us but still wish my family wasn't so Kim Butter wouldn't be trying to avoid them not to even talk to my family.

The work week went well as we continued to save and looking at more apartments until we finally found the one Kim Butter liked close to Saymen Avenue on fourteen street and we checked it out. It was nice apartment and we had to jump on it before it was taken so we put hold money of $100 on it to have the rest of first month and last month rent. Heading home was happy times for us that now together we are getting a place as a couple but then she asked the wrong question. Kim Butter wanted to still tell my parents of our relationship and I couldn't avoid it so I had no choice but to call them. As I was dialing their number was praying at same time line be busy but mom picked up saying who is this just as rude as ever and what you want. I just said hi how is everybody and just came out said I am now seeing Kim Butter we are a couple and she like to meet yall. My mother still became upset but then Kim Butter took the phone and I could tell my mother was telling her things but she was calm and said that while she respects the family, Daire is a grown man and can make my own decisions and still hung up nice saying good night. Kim Butter still was mad but didn't let my parents stop us from being together and that was all God.

Still as we relaxed trying to get ready to move to new place my parents then started to call and bother us but we still made sure they didn't bother us anymore as we had to take phone off hook middle of night and then fell asleep in each other arms.

Through the month of April and May she talked to her family a lot and one day her sister Lanna stopped by to see her and she was nice as Kim Butter let her in and I introduced myself as Daire. I said it's nice to meet you and I really care about your sister as Lanna said okay. Kim Butter told her we have plans to move at the end of May to new place and Lanna smiled and said nice to meet you and Kim Butter walked her outside as I knew this family is close and caring.

Things were looking up for us as we made it thru another week to finally saved enough money to move and was ready to do that on this last month of May that Friday to move into our new apartment. So, that Friday evening Kim Butter had asked her that father and brother came over after work to help us move the big stuff to the apartment. It was nice seeing her brother Rooney as he hugged her and said hi to me and I said nice to meet you. I helped him with the bed and the rest of the furniture up and down the long steps while her father Hoard was relaxing in the van. We managed to get everything moved from the old apartment to the new apartment on Saymen Avenue. Then still had to that night wipe down and clean the old apartment as best we could so no issues. As we finally got done moving to the new apartment her brother Rooney and Mr. Hoard shook my hand and reminded me to take diligent care of his sister and Mr. Hoard daughter. And it still felt good knowing I have a new family that really cares and together help each of that I never ever had with my family I have now with Kim Butter. As we were tired from moving that we just left things everywhere and went to sleep together that it was a good day with peace.

The next day we woke up in our new couple bless apartment and she really liked the apartment we had a nice little kitchen and our bedroom was separated from rest of the apartment with a nice sized living room too. We cleaned this place up and then got a chance to relaxed with the nice and cozy place and she wanted to buy little stuff to match throughout the apartment.

It was Monday back to work as we woke up happy together in our new apartment got dress caught trolley together walking down the street holding each other hands until we got to the station. I thanked God for the huge blessing that my life had become he turned it around for my good.

Later thru week decided to get a new phone to use and it was nice but as soon as we connected it of course my family was calling with it having caller ID on it so we can know who is calling and answering machine too. Things were starting to go nice and smoothly for us but of course we would get my silly parents calling as that father called saying he wanted to meet Kim Butter and I took it as not good but did talk to him saying I will let you know when we will come up there and hung up quickly. Still trying to enjoy our time together with new place that we even went out to celebrate by dancing for the first time we out Saturday night at a nice club called the Pluto. What a wonderful time and I was so, so lucky to be with Kim Butter looking so beautiful as we continued to dance the night away and then later went home happy together.

Then Sunday we chilled at home and I thought that I had to let her know my parents wanted to meet her. So, I told her but Kim Butter was not happy about that and we argued because she didn't like them how they treated me when I first lived with her for those two days at old apartment. But had to explain to her that I wanted to get past them so we can move on with our lives.

Finally, we came to an agreement where we could respect both my family as well as our relationship and decided to work together and still see my parents get it over with. Later I called my parents my mom answered rude as ever who is this and I said it's me Daire we would like to come over on a Saturday is that okay as mom yelled on phone to that father asking him and he said ok so I said okay bye and quickly hung up. Knowing how far they live we had to call for price of getting on the bus to Jersy Transit which was an hour ride. Thru the weeks and month of June I was just praying and praying God get us thru this meeting my family and back home safely while at work we had a great easy work week me and Kim Butter. Then it was Friday night and we got home rested a we talked about not to get into no arguments with my parents and I would not look at that father mean just keep praying. In the evening we had nice dinner and went to bed early getting rest for tomorrow's carnival with my family. The next day we woke up to get ready for the event of Kim Butter meeting my family as I was praying things go well. So, I said good morning to Kim Butter as she said am I ready to meet my parents and I said yes want to get this over with. We got dress around 10am and needed to get downtown by 12pm to catch that Traveler Bus to New Jersey by 12:20pm because it's an hour ride. Heading out together locking the apartment and made it to catch the trolley we sat together still happy no matter what might happen. Made it downtown to Marred street toward Traveler and just got there at 12:10pm to get on bus and a nice seat together. It was a smooth ride with the windows tinted that Kim Butter fell asleep while I stayed awake for our stop in Burlington. We finally got there and I woke Kim Butter up telling her we here the bus dropped us off at the plaza so we got out and I went to a payphone to call my parents. My mom answered said all fake hi and I said we here at the plaza so she had that father come pick us up and I was getting ready for his fake ways too. The area is okay but not much stores as we waited about 20 minutes before that father showed up waving seeing us. He got out the car hugging Kim Butter all fake said hi nice to meet you and then shook my hand said hi son phony that father but we got into the car heading to the house. He asked while driving where Kim Butter live at and she said West Pricard all quick of course rude but she kept her beautiful smile as I was getting mad still. We got there and mother opened the door saying hi to Kim Butter and then she met the rest of the family showing off another rented house they can't afford as Bernadette and Kevin was there. So, we sat on couch as mom was asking all kinds of questions about how we met and stuff just all in our business like where Kim Butter parents live as she told them with no worries and I was trying to hold her nice and relax way. Later we were watching the TV and then it was time to eat we had pizza at the table and then here it happened that father started saying rude things like what yall like candle lite couple now comments. I was smiling but inside was upset trying my best support and defend Kim Butter at the table and things wasn't getting any better feeling it time to leave. Still, we finished eating dinner spaghetti as it became quiet all the sudden for a change. Then sat in the living room watching some movie that father put in the a dvd player but I was ready to go so me and Kim Butter said its late we must catch our bus. My mom said nice meeting you Kim Butter as she hugged her and I said bye to Bernadette and Kevin then to mom. We headed into the car that father took us back to the bus stop but could see Kim Butter face was upset and knew she had a lot to say when we get home. It was a quiet ride to the bus terminal as that father drop us off and I said bye he hugged Kim Butter said nice meeting you laughing but nothing was funny. As he drove off then she told me my parents are so disrespectful to me and you didn't say anything but sit there smiling and I said sorry but it was too late. I knew I was going to have a bad ride home with Kim Butter trying to talk about it but she was so upset at my family that I couldn't calm her down all the way home. She said my family was so rude to her and I didn't stand up to them enough that she was about to tell my parents off herself and that I didn't want. Once we were home, she called her that father and told him everything that had happened upset and mad. Then later we talked and I just kept apologizing to Kim Butter about how rude and ignorant my parents are but she still was not hearing it as I just left her alone.

Her that father came over later to the apartment and took me outside to his car to talk telling me I needed to be a man and stand up for the one I love and not back down. It was the truth and had nothing else to say to Mr. Hoard but I love Kim Butter and won't let that happen again and he shook my hand and I went back into the apartment still leaving Kim Butter alone. That day was the worst day I could ever had imagined and rest of the weekend she was quiet with no conversation what so ever and I prayed and ask God to please keep this relationship together that What God Put Together Let Nothing Separate Us.

On Monday month of July at work I told the guys what happened and they said I needed to stand up for Kim Butter that they did the same thing Sufon and Lanley for their wives. It helped a lot to talk to them and now is not the time to care about my parent's feelings when I have a relationship with Kim Butter that I love and need to show it. So, on lunch break I decided to call my parent's and my mother pick up the phone as I said hi need to tell yall how much the family had upset Kim Butter and that father was rude to her not rite. My mother started yelling like so what and then that father got on the phone for what reason I don't know just talking about calm down but still being smart saying he didn't like her and that's was it as I was about to tell him off he done to me but was at work so hung up quick and still angry going home knowing I can't let them mess up my first time safe happiness no more.

When I got home tried talking to Kim Butter hoping she forgive me when everything came out as telling her I told my parents off and you are important to me not be scared but stand up to them because I love you. She still wasn't happy so to make things better planned to take her out to movies and dinner hoping she forgive me and we celebrate the 4th of July together in a happy way.

She said okay as we were getting dress to go but then got a phone call from her family that her brother was sick and had to go to the hospital from falling down the steps outside. Kim Butter was so upset as I tried to calm her down as we went to the hospital quickly and got there but had to wait for the doctors to let us see him. Later we were able to see him as Kim Butter went in first saying hi hugging him with Mr. and Mrs. Hoard in the room glad he is okay but still needed rest. I then came in said he brother glad you alright and get ready for me to beat you in some football no excuses. Rooney laughed and it was good to see so I gave him hug as Kim Butter hugged her brother saying get well soon as we let him get rest with the medicine doctors about to give him for pain. Mr. and Mrs. Hoard said thank you for coming as me and Kim Butter left out happy.

Kim Butter told me she was thankful for my support to her brother and family as it was what I suppose to do especially with a family to care and respect me so, we went back home happier then when we came here. Toward the weekend Rooney got out of the hospital and got safely home with his family and then later that week Kim Butter and me went to her family house to see him as he recovered quickly back to his normal self so we played games together that's when I knew the real brother outside of my family was Rooney.

Going back to work I was feeling better with things between Kim Butter and me as we started to get back to that closeness in our relationship. Still doing good at my job tried to call my parents at work but that father answered the phone and I didn't want to hear it just hung up phone on him. I got home that night ready to relax and Kim Butter as she came at me saying she love me and that was a remarkable thing to come home too. For the next couple of weeks we enjoyed ourselves with nothing but peaceful happiness as she planned to give me a nice birthday with just us on July 23rd. Knowing home was good it helped me not try to talk to my parents but let God handle them and stay focus on what God is making work which is Kim Butter and me. Then that day came for me it was my birthday and woke up to a beautiful Kim Butter giving me a kiss singing happy birthday to me had a card for me too was all I could ever ask or need. What an enjoyable day like never before with her as she fixed me breakfast and I had a wonderful time. Still early in morning her family called to wish me a happy birthday too was so, so nice to receive that I was crying full of joy from a real caring family. It was a wonderful birthday still going to work as I got there my co-workers wished me happy birthday too that made it a momentous day to be here. Finally, ready to get home quickly not knowing what Kim Butter has planned for me came into the apartment and saw a birthday cake as she was dress so, so nice for saying she has plans to take me out to movies too making it the best birthday ever!

Then it was back to work but still enjoying my great birthday with Kim Butter as I got to work focus and happy with Malandy and Rocco but then got a call from that father at work telling me that Terance and Jevone were no longer at the old house and that Jevone was marrying his girlfriend and that was the only reason I took the call but still hung up. As I got home and relaxed with Kim Butter we then talked about the day and then told her my brothers Terance and Jevone aren't at the house anymore at Philly and Jevone is talking about marriage with his girlfriend. She was happy for my brother and then said she wants to get married too. It made me ready to let Kim Butter into my world of abuse and being molested not sure if she still be with me to love me enough with a future together. We enjoyed our summer together thru August into September as I started talking to guy friends Lanley and Sufon at work to see how they found their future wife in their lives. They told me you know in your heart that this is the one for you and not question it but just do what's good for both of yall happiness. With work ending I started thinking and feeling in my heart with no doubt that Kim Butter is the love of my life and will do everything to not lose what God bless me with. As I got in the apartment went rite to Kim Butter kissing her telling her I love her then went home did what I needed to do loving her, cooking and told her how happy I am we are together.

As we enjoyed our loving times together in September and in meantime, I did call my brother Jevone wishing him happy birthday and congratulations on him and his Fiancee to talked to him about how he knew she was the one. Jevone just said it felt rite and he never experienced it before but knew this was something that he didn't want to lose. I was glad for him and hoping I get to feel and do the same for me and Kim Butter while I told Jevone good luck talk to you later and had to do for me now. During the week at work it just hit me to now put aside money to buy a ring for Kim Butter.

Making this decision to put money aside felt great as I started looking downtown hoping to find a nice ring place and not miss any sales going on. I started to work hard and do overtime staying late to finish other projects just to get extra money to get Kim Butter her ring. The months went by fast with no silly or rude parents calling me at home or work was a remarkable thing. Plus, Thanksgiving was coming up and Kim Butter had already planned for us to go to her parent' house for dinner so I was happy about that.

At work my coworkers talked about this week of Thanksgiving would be the men cooking for the family was nice to hear but I was just looking for being around happy family like Kim Butter knowing my family don't even appreciated not one family time together.

As Thanksgiving Day was here it was nice weather not too cold as me and Kim Butter got up had nice breakfast and relaxed watching the Thanksgiving Parades on tv. She later called her parents wishing them Happy Thanksgiving and so did I then we cleaned up the place a little got dress and caught the bus to get to her house for the dinner. It was a comfortable ride because hardly nobody was on the bus and made it there in 1hr as we got to door her that father let us in and I shook his hand saying hi Mr. Hoard and to Mrs. Hoard, then to

Rooney and rest of family was nice too. With it not yet 5pm for dinner I went to Rooney room to play some games with him like football was nice to do. While Kim Butter was downstairs with her mother and rest sister and family fixing Thanksgiving Dinner and table set up. I beat her brother once and he beat me was fun doing as it was then time for dinner and we came downstairs sat at table and prayed having a nice Thanksgiving Dinner with her family something I never had with mines. The food was so good we had some to take home as I hugged her parents and siblings saying thank you had a fun time as me and Kim Butter was going to catch the bus home but her that father gave us a ride home. Mr. Hoard got us home and we said good bye headed into the apartment with the food and I told Kim Butter what a nice wonderful Thanksgiving with her family for me and enjoyed rest of our night together. Heading back to work was nice too with my coworkers Lanley, Sufon saying their Thanksgiving was nice and so did Malandy and Rocco talk about theirs good too. Then at work we started to work on making Christmas signs so I knew we was just around the corner for Christmas. There was a lot of work needed to be done it was good for me because I needed the extra money to put on Kim Butter ring to hopefully have it out by the time of her birthday would be so, so nice. Kim Butter also was working overtime too knowing she had to get gifts for her niece and nephews as well. The past three weeks all we did was just come home and get rest not much going out too tired from working. Plus, with my brother Jevone planning for his wedding next year in July had me so focus on Kim Butter to be my Fiancee too. Afterwork Kim Butter and I would meet downtown at the toy stores in the gallery to get for her niece and nephew gifts before Christmas while I was still trying to figure out what to get Kim Butter since I still didn't have enough funds for her real gift her ring. So, thought of a substitute to buy her a nice sweater and made sure to tell her how much I love her hoping she still be happy with this Christmas gift.

Things started to feel great with this week of work Christmas Eve and Day coming I felt much happier than ever being before. Knowing I come home to peaceful caring woman in Kim Butter made this Christmas and New Year's Eve much more special. As I worked hard on completing our Holiday signs at work with Malandy and Rocco we did excellent job that finished the job 2 days before Christmas Eve. As I headed home Kim Butter was there and we hugged I asked her how was her day she said busy and we relaxed and had nice dinner of pork chops she cooked and was good. Later went to bed and slept good waking up to Christmas Eve was a day of early leaving good for us as we got dress headed to work. I had a light day with projects done everybody in good mood saying Merry Christmas and time flew by fast less people working as others had off too. By time I knew it was time to go home I said bye and have a great Christmas to everybody hurrying up to meet Kim Butter so we could go to pick up the rest of the gifts at the stores for her family and my gift for her too. By time we got home it was late and we just crashed but still had to wrapped the gifts up and mines so later woke up and did that then fell asleep. The next day was Christmas Day as we woke up and I hugged and kissed her say Merry Christmas with it after nine in the morning as her family called wishing us a Merry Christmas too. Then my family fake call saying Merry Christmas as Kim Butter and I said thanks quickly hanging up knowing we don't have time for any nonsense on this day. Before we left out and had talked about me going over my family house after going to see her family first then we exchange gifts and I gave her mines she opened it but with a little smile. It looked like she was expecting what I couldn't get at the time her ring but still said thanks with some disappointment. I felt bad but hope she still Wait and Be Patient and of Good Courage Knowing It Will all Work Out According to God's Purpose For Us.

She then gave me my gift was nice dockers and sweater to match in blue my favorite color as I hugged and kiss her saying thank you. Still seeing her not happy about her gift she said it would have been nicer if you gave me a ring as we were heading out and I apologize stating I didn't have enough money but will make it up to you. As we got to her family house with the presents everybody was so, so nice hugging me saying Merry Christmas like the type of family

I always wanted unlike mines. It was great to see her niece and nephews so happy as her mother, that father, brother, and sisters were too exchanging gifts what a nice family to be with God put me to be a part of. As we enjoyed ourselves, I had to go to my family house unfortunately and didn't want to leave but said I be back then headed out still happy. By the time getting to my parent's house in New Jersey took 2 ½ hours got there said hi to my mother and that father with Bernadette and Kevin wish them Merry Christmas. I had presents for them and only bought mother and that father hat and gloves as Jevone was there and I said hi but no Terance hoping he okay. I only stayed for hour knowing I must get back to be with Kim Butter but of course they didn't really ask about her knew that would happen. Later had something to eat as Jevone was ready to go be with his Fiancee soon to be wife as mother and that father didn't like her but he didn't care and left as I hugged him saying see yah. Knowing I wasn't about to be there by myself left 30 minutes after said bye got to get home its late and hug mother, Bernadette and Kevin as that father just said bye. Was so glad to get out of that fake caring parents running to catch the bus back to Philadelphia to be with my real happiness family. As I got my bus and relaxed almost feel asleep with the long ride made it back to Kim Butter family house as she was ready to go had a great time and we hugged her family leaving out with her parents giving us money was nice gift too. Getting home she was smiling happy and so was I not talking much about my visit to my family she just asked was I okay going there and I said yes. As we got home just dropped everything and went rite to bed knowing tomorrow that we still must go back to work but at least with something happy to talk about as I hope Kim Butter will still know she will have her ring on next year.

Back to work I worked hard and was doing my best to save for a ring because don't like to say one thing and not follow thru knowing Kim Butter deserve it and I love her more than just a girlfriend but my Fiancee. With this short week as well, there wasn't much work needed to be done except the New Year signs and that was not hard jobs for us in the Sign Shop. A lot of people was off this week as well that been at the job over 10 years. So, with work no pressure the week was quickly going by that before we knew it work on New Year's Eve day was so smooth and light that it felt like half a day as I said Happy New Year to my coworkers and ran out to get home to Kim Butter. Looking forward to going into the New Year with my love of my life, friend and soon to be Fiancee in 1993. She had already got home and I just kissed her at the door saying I love her and can't wait to celebrate the New Year with you as she smiled and we relaxed.

Later the evening we got some glasses together and she bought some coolers for us to drink was great as we watched tv on the events for the night. All excited like little kids Kim Butter and I was getting pulp up as the time flew fast and count down was coming as we waited up. Then we said, "5, 4,3,2,1 Happy New Year 1993" kissed, hugged, and drank to a new happy as one together couple. Kim Butter then called her family and wish them Happy New Year too and I also did. I prayed that God would keep us together that What God Put Together Let Nothing Separate.

The next day was so different feeling that I never felt before peace and happiness with Kim Butter and this New Year for us that even going back to work was different. We left out went to work as I said bye to my future wife heading to my job and was glad to see my coworkers as they had enjoyed their time with family. The work week was busy with the New Year that there was overtime still and that I needed. So, the week went fast as Friday I got paid and went across to Wittin and Celary walking in an out of stores looking for a nice engagement ring. When finally, I saw it the one so went to put $75 down to hold it and knew Kim Butter would love.

Plus, things were looking up through the month of January with me getting the extra money I needed at work that every time I got paid was putting money on Kim Butter's ring and it felt good too. She also was having good weeks at work with her job giving her overtime too.

Still staying focus I hadn't talked to my family since Christmas Eve decided to just call make sure they okay and found out from mother that Jevone was getting married in July. But, of course she wasn't happy and neither was that father but I didn't care was happy for my brother and said okay bye hanging up quickly. Later as I got home to Kim Butter discussed me calling my parents and about Jevone getting married she was happy as thought about us going to his wedding would be nice using our income tax money and rite there I knew she deserve that ring.

While working hard thru January into February came, I had plans to give her the ring soon like on her birthday be perfect. But, then began putting money aside for Valentine's Day gifts also still having $70 for her ring each paycheck. At home Kim Butter was cooking dinner for me every night spaghetti or Salisbury Steak and to see my future wife cook was so nice. During the week one day she asked me am I getting her a nice Valentine's Day Gift and just said can't tell you and don't worry you will like it as she gave me that look like talk is cheap. Still couldn't wait to show Kim Butter the preview of this Valentine Day Gift of what I really, really must give to her on her birthday will be wonderful.

The day was now here and what a day to wake up to as I kissed Kim Butter saying Happy Valentine's Day. Little did she know that I was coming to her job with a shocking surprise that she never expected. Later we hugged and kissed but still had to get to work and I told her I love her on the trolley kissing her all the way to work before leaving her. When I got to work told my coworkers my plans to surprise Kim Butter and they said cool!

It was such a great feeling of love on me that nothing anybody could say or do to me would take my happy love I have for Kim Butter. So, I was getting my work done quickly by going to lunch on time to give her Valentine's Day Gift at her job. So, had to get the gifts and then get on the trolley to her job at Highten and market with people all looking at me mad and some smiling as I was so excited couldn't wait to see Kim Butter face. By the time I got there walking up the steps to cross the street to her job came to the front desk and asked to call for Kim Butter Hoard to come down to the entrance. Standing there in the lobby as people was looking at me knowing she is about to come off the elevator then it happened I saw her as Kim Butter was so, so surprised. I kissed her said I love you, Happy Valentine's Day and gave her the balloons, card, and candy as she just stood there so happy and kissed me again saying thank you love you and took the gifts back to her job to work. I was so happy leaving knowing that she deserves all the love from me because I never been so happy in love in a long, long time and thank God for this.

Later she called me at work and said she love me and I was smiling from ear to ear the rest of the day couldn't wait to get home to my loving soon to be Fiancee. We had such a romantic Valentines night like never before that will always remember how much we are meant to be together. With so much love in the air between us that thru the rest of February everyday was Valentine's day. Then also I was getting more excited about only owing $200 on her ring ready to have it soon.

With work project I was getting done deadlines because March was a busy month for me at work of sales and discount signs had to be made with each week. Still coming home was so, so great as Kim Butter was spending time talking to her family making sure they okay and I would just relax get rest. Then decided to call my family don't know why but just to check on my sister Bernadette and Kevin okay. As Kim Butter made dinner I ate and she was talking to her girlfriends about what I gave her for Valentine's Day still was great to hear while I went to bed early. As I went to work next day on lunch, I happen to call my parents for checkup and found out from mother that Jevone wanted me to be his best man.

My parents still were not happy about Jevone getting married as mother said she not going and then that father tried to talk to me for what like fake that father asking me how I am doing as I just said fine got to go and hung up. Later left the job and got home to Kim Butter to tell her my brother Jevone wants me to be his best man and she was like that is nice but you must rent a tuxedo and we talk about budgeting that to happen during the night. In the meantime, the next couple of weeks working was that I had to make double work with this March Sales week of work signs needed to be done. It helped a lot with my paycheck because I got the payment for Kim Butter ring down from $200 to only owing $70 and next week's check would do it so I couldn't get tired when I needed this overtime money. Still just coming home as Kim Butter was tired too working that we relaxed ate dinner and went to bed on time. With one week left before Kim Butter birthday I had to make sure my check was enough to get the ring out, take her out to dinner and pay bills too that I not come up short. When I got paid that Friday just had enough money to do everything I needed and went to the jewelry to get my Fiancee ring out with all smiles afterwork. When I saw it was so happy asked them to please clean it as they did respectable job and put it in a nice box for me too. I went home making sure nothing happens to Kim Butter's ring heading straight home quickly. As I got home, she was there saying it was a busy day for her and I said just rest as I went to hide her Fiancee ring away safe place and made my own dinner later going to sleep rite with my love. During her birthday week I thought to ask her parents of a lovely place to take Kim Butter out on her birthday as Mr. And Mrs. Hoard suggested to take her out at downtown restaurant. So, later looked up some on the internet and was lucky to find one with good and affordable prices a place called Casper Restaurant and Berbin Street.

I made the reservations for us at night 8pm and was excited for our night planned as the next day That Wednesday I told Kim Butter we have plans to go out on your birthday to a nice restaurant and she was little surprised but happy. Still enjoying the rest of the week of beautiful times together in a happy blessed way she was getting her clothes together for our night out and I was too.

Then, it was here our special day and Kim Butter Birthday as I woke up singing to her Happy Birthday as she was excited with me kissing her and having a sweet card telling Kim Butter that I will fix breakfast for her. As we were enjoying our time celebrating her family called wishing her Happy Birthday and they talked. Then her friends called her too which was nice to know they didn't forget her birthday either. Later we chilled and I had finally told her I have reservations at The Casper Restaurant for her birthday at 7pm and Kim Butter was so happy hugging and kissing me couple times. She later got ready to look nice for our night out and so did I just couldn't wait to really give Kim Butter the gift I been longing to give her. As we got ready to go out, I looked at her so, so, beautiful staring for a few minutes almost forget what time it was as we had to go it was after 5:30 in the evening. We still had to catch the trolley but made it and found a seat together with Kim Butter smiling from ear to ear as the weather was a nice night for us. Our timing getting to downtown was good we got there at 6:40 still had time to walk to the restaurant in love and got there okay to Robs Restaurant as I open the door for my future Fiancee and said our name for reservations for two and was seated with a nice table. The waiter gave us the menus and time to look it over as Kim Butter and I was looking at how nice this place was for our first time here. As the waiter came back, I let Kim Butter order first her dinner and drink then I picked mines too. Still Kim Butter was so excited while I was going into my pocket to get the ring box out on the chair underneath so she doesn't see it. Then our food was served to us as we were eating, I was getting little nervous because didn't want to mess it up giving her the Fiancee ring and saying the words wrong so I asked God to help me say the this right to Kim Butter. As we enjoyed our dinner then I told the waiter it's her birthday today so after we finished eating, they brought out a nice ice cream cake for her singing Happy Birthday to you, Happy Birthday to you, Happy Birthday Kim Butter, Happy Birthday to you. She was so happy smiling then I knew it was time as I got the box with the ring in my left hand and grabbed her right hand with my right hand on one knee in front of her opened the box with the engagement ring and said, "I love you Kim Butter you mean the world to me, I want to spend the rest of my life with you will you marry me?." She almost choked on the cake in shock and then said, Yes, I will marry you!." She kissed me and hugged me and everyone in the restaurant was clapping as she kissed and hugged me again. I began to cry never thought to be here doing this but god kept me alive for this day. As she took rest of her cake to go and kept looking at her ring as we walking catch trolley so happy that I told her it was time to show you how much more you are to me that we are meant to be together rest of our lives in marriage and she just cried again kissing me asking me how you do this. Just told her I was looking for a while and found nice jewelry place downtown and was saving for it past 6 months still giving you money to pay the bills and because you can budget and help a lot that you didn't even question my check. Plus, I told you was paying off my loan for school and you trust me as she just kept looking at her ring saying it beautiful and couldn't wait to tell her family as while we were loving each other all way home and then made it there as the first thing she did was call her parents. It was after 9pm so excited that hoping they weren't sleeping her mom still picked up the phone and she just let it out mom Daire gave me engagement ring for my birthday at restaurant got on one knee and we are getting married screaming as she continued to tell rest of her family calling everybody including her girlfriends while I was so happy that she is my fiancée knowing my future always been with her. So, this went on for hours but some of her girlfriends didn't seem excited as she still didn't let that stop her still on phone telling them detail after detail where we went how I did it and so on that by time she was done talking it was after 1am and I was waiting patiently though still had plans to call my parents and tell them tomorrow not ruin our night. So, then after she finished talking it was our time and we had a loving each other thru the rest of the night with Kim Butter looking at her ring saying its beautiful you got good taste almost not sleeping as we made love then finally went to bed. The next day was more plans that Sunday to go to her parent's house and show them so we did wake up later that day loving still going on but before we left to go out, I had to call my parents and tell them whether they receive it or not can't disrespect her not telling my family. So, I asked god make this phone call peaceful called my mom she picked up saying what is it Kim Butter birthday yesterday tell her happy birthday as I said she said thank you but I have something to tell yall. Knowing my mother as she overreacted said is she pregnant and I said no told her I gave Kim Butter an engagement ring over her birthday dinner last night we getting married as she just didn't say anything but okay why and I knew this is going to be bad. I tried to not let Kim Butter hear that as she just took the phone saying hi Mrs. Cylence, I am so happy and love your son want to marry him he is a good man as mom just said okay congratulation in a not happy way. Then she just said yelling to that dad that Daire has something to tell you he got on the phone, I said me, and Kim Butter are getting married I gave her engagement ring over dinner last night she accepted as he was like okay happy for you but not so then Kim Butter got the phone said thank you and Daire is a great man and I love him very much as that dad didn't say much but then she gave me phone and I just said hope yall be happy for us love yall and I just hung up. I knew that they would act so rude to her but I did my best to not let it mess up our joy we have as Kim Butter still said they really mad at us now but I don't care so we got ready and left to spend time over her family house that respect us. We still left and made it over to there as Kim Butter parent's said congratulations to her but her sister was little happy while her brother was happy as we relaxed over there and her dad was like now you get ready for what living with someone for rest of your life trying to make me laugh and he did too. It was nice and great to be welcomed like that but not get that from my own parents as we continued to celebrated at her parent's house for a while still her second oldest sister was still in shock but happy so then we had to leave as her parents told all her relatives and that was good to hear we then left heading home and she was just all over me we holding hands going home took the trolley home instead of having her dad take us home he tired. That was a great weekend for us and we got home loving again each other like we were already married but then there was all these phone messeges from my parents and my younger brother too which I forgot to tell as he was happy for us but of course my parents left something silly like why now and other things but she quickly erased it. As that great weekend was over then as we went to work that week Kim Butter really got a lot of attention showing off her engagement ring to her coworkers as some was happy others were jealous and at my job it was congratulations but some were not happy for me like why she wanted to marry me but I laughed it off. It was a fun week and that continued for a while as people still was in shock that me and Kim Butter are getting married like she can do better than me and it bothered me but I kept smiling as we started to plan for next year's wedding and she was already ahead of me but we were still saving to get that car to have plus make it to Jevone wedding too. So, we were talking about when and what church and then about taking a trip too because we weren't just getting married and not do a nice honeymoon trip for us so she had people at her job that she talked to about saving for the trip too and I thought to do all the work man I am marrying the rite woman. As the weeks went by fast from both of our heads spinning with people just calling wishes us congratulations but not from my side only hers then she was starting to budget and said she tell me soon what place and how much and the date too because she not going to be engaged another year as I just said yes dear.

20

FACING ADVERSITY
TO NEW PATH

H ad a chance to talk to Jevone after work during that second
week of April as he was coming back 2 months from getting
married telling me he knew she was the one for him and I
better know that too as saying I do as we talked for a while more that
Wednesday night about our messy parents saying they not coming
while Kim Butter was resting from all the excitement at work with
people coming up to her that didn't even speak to her about being
engaged. Jevone was telling me to get ready for the smart remarks to
make me upset but don't stop so I finally got off the phone said talk
to you later brother and went to bed with my fiancée it was so
wonderful to know that no matter how it's been with my family she
still said yes not knowing everything but saw my heart wants to love
her and she will get that love back. While she was getting our
wedding plans for next year together that I was still looking to get
that car for us so I talked to the man about putting money down and
we wanted it too but didn't want to lose this car because we need one.
As I was working, I did notice my coworker Malandy was not as
happy I guess she wish her man would give her a ring but tried to
hide it though as I couldn't help her with that but still, she was still

in shock that we are getting married because she knew Kim Butter before me. The day was going good I then started to think about my family that they will never accept any of their kid's decision to leave and I must stop trying to be a peacemaker and just live my life now or loose Kim Butter and I don't want that to happen. Then as I got home that night from work my fiancée was telling me she made some calls to check out a wedding dress and then wanted us to start saving for a trip to Florida that I was happy to hear I don't have a lazy fiancée as I told her that we can still get that car too with our income tax coming this weekend too before somebody else get it. We talked all thru the night planning for our future wedding together because now is the time as we then went to bed finally with still her family calling her in shock that she getting married and is the youngest girl too. The weekend was here and in the mail was our income tax money rite on time so we can cash it the Monday into the bank and we both got something good back so we then started to budget what we spend and put away for the wedding too so as the planning continued thru the weekend with us going places to look at wedding dresses and stuff. We headed out downtown to couple stores finally one she liked trying on wedding dresses so soon but nothing like the present though I couldn't be there to see it as I was checking out suit for me to wear too and it was a fun time for both of us that we went back home so excited as Kim Butter was also getting her girlfriends to meet her downtown to help her too. Still can't believe this is happening for me as work week was here again and this April shower month almost over I had to talk to Jevone with 2 months to go and get my best man suit also for his wedding too so at home I called him asking what colors should I be wearing and he told me then asked me am I ready to do marriage and I said yeah just like you are as we laughed talking for a while that night but I had to get off the phone Kim Butter needed to call her people as she said congratulations to my brother and his fiancée saying we rite behind yall. That week was nothing but going places after work as we decided to go buy a car with us putting savings away and check out couple places as I made phone calls. While enjoying our celebration I had finally found a place cheap car for $1500 but only $400 down so I talked to Kim Butter and she trusted me as we got our money out from bank and seeing what we work on first so we decided to get that car and planned to get it that following Saturday so that was plan. I then had a phone call that Friday when we was home from my messy parents always yelling saying Daire pick up pick up I know you there with Kim Butter pick up so I just finally did saying hi but of course mom was in her mood saying did I talk to Jevone and I said yes I going to be his best man as she still not going being mean and threatening me too as I tried to not get on her bad said but now is not the time to take sides. After that painful talk with my parents I had to calm down because I was Upset as Kim Butter was rite there saying you got to stop letting them talk to you like that and I just didn't say anything but agree as rest of the night we talked about our wedding and that nothing is going to stop us from getting married not even your parents so I felt better and we tried to enjoy our Friday nite for us by turning off the voicemail still able to see who is calling then pick up. As we still enjoyed our weekend to go pick up that nice car before we got up early with the money needed to buy the car excited and glad that we finally will have one. Before we left, Kim Butter fixed us a nice eggs and bacon she learned cook good from her mom and then we left out on our way talking she saw at a woman store nice outfit to wear to Jevone wedding that later within 3 months before my brother wedding which was also my birthday month too. We had to catch two things to get there about 1 ½ hours and had an exciting time smiling on the bus too talking about her family still shocked she is really getting married while I had nothing good to say about mines. All I could do was listen to her talk that by the time she was done we was walking down toward the dealership. I was hoping and praying that car is still there and by time we got there I saw it a block away with my 20/20 vision happy then we went inside talk to the dealer and did all paperwork that hours later we shook hands as Kim Butter looked at it again and was happy with nice clean car our first together. So, as I was nervous but still okay drove that car as I had gotten my license while ago but didn't have a car to drive and Kim Butter didn't have a license so as we leaving he gave us directions to get back onto expressway back home and I was nervous about that but still told me I must get some full coverage insurance for the car because he gave me temporary insurance of 30 days then after that we on our own. So, we put our seat belts on and went driving it was great but I had to be careful because it's been long time since I had been behind the wheel of a car since living with my parents as this was a learning lesson that took us about 2 hours just to get home with both of us being nervous getting on expressway the first time. I was so scared that I stayed in the right lane all way home driving only 30 miles hours worried somebody hit us with Kim Butter yelling all way there watch that car, move over or too fast that what scared me not the road but her constantly talking. By the time it got better was when we came up the rap toward Wardin street she then was little better but still talking and then finally we were there as I remembered how to park with her hitting my hazards lights like so then I found spot rite in front of our apartment sweating like I was running a marathon. We got out and all we did was look at our nice car happy then I wanted to just go to bed rest while she locked the door and we made it thank goodness so then rest of that day we accomplished something else now having a car to go places and for Jevone wedding too not depending on my messy parents who don't want us to be there anyway but we going. We were so glad to make it home with our new car because that was it to us a new car event though it was ten years old but it was ours. Then later Kim Butter had called her parents tell them we bought that car and they were so happy for us that wanted us to come over tomorrow Sunday to show them because I didn't have anybody to celebrate with so might as well enjoy it with her family. Later we ate and enjoyed a quiet Saturday night relaxing because I was drained from driving all way here for the first time went to bed early but still went outside check on our car as she said we need to buy a car club to lock the car so nobody can steal it. Kim Butter always thinks ahead and that is why I marrying her because she looks out for us as I said okay we can buy one as we went back in apartment to sleep and enjoy this time that was a terrific way to start this weekend on a good note. Following that Sunday as we still didn't do anything on Sunday but relax and headed over her parents house as she gave me the direction shortcut there but stopped off at Body Fixer Shop that she showed me to get a car club and was then headed over their house. It was a great feeling though to be around them again as her dad was checking it out saying it's nice and her mom too with rest of family so we chilled there again for a while then later left out heading home carefully and she said thank you for spending time with my family and brother they like you and I said hope. We got home later putting that car club on and that was enough for me with a weekend we both enjoyed and accomplish some things too that all she talked about is she can't wait to marry me and I her too not let nothing stop us whether people accept it or not because to marry her is a love that I know is forever. That weekend we had a great time it was then back to work that following week with having a car now helped a lot but we didn't really use it for our jobs because I had no parking spots and Kim Butter job was too expensive because all she catch is the trolley anyway. The only time we use it was going food shopping and out for ourselves that we did do during the work week as I did tell my coworkers I had a used car and they were happy for me Malandy said is Kim Butter driving yet and I said no she doesn't know how to yet but she wants to. Then we go see her parents that Wednesday see how they doing and it was great to not have to catch trolley so as the weekend came and we decided to go out this time dancing to lovely place downtown. We had to pay for parking that this club was our first time here but her girlfriends at job told her it's nice because they had an upper lever tables that we relaxed at as I had just soda and she had a rum and coke watching each other. Then one of our favorite dance songs came on "We Came Here To Kick Boots" and it was on like popcorn because me and Kim Butter love to dance we was kicking it all night. All I know is that on my list of things I love for my future wife have is able to dance which is in the top 5 and she wasn't shy about dancing either that she can pop like me too man it was beautiful we were sweating it out of our clothes and left when it was over. That what made my love for her so strong that she didn't let my family issues stop her from still seeing a future with me and my deep past issues. We headed home and it was start of our new life together full of fun, joy, and happiness that I can't wait to call her Mrs. Cylence. Now time to get car insurance too that was money but we still found a way with Kim Butter budgeting all bills to have gas food for us to eat thank god. It was a great few weeks with the car that we were taking it to movies and then seeing her family too taking her mom store so it help them too as it was also April showers and having car kept us dry. Then heading into May my job was good didn't have any problems but still parents bothering me at work calling mom tried to upset me saying I shouldn't go to Jevone wedding and they be against me if I do as I just tried to talk nice while coworkers looking on. By time I got off I still said love yall and got to go so I could go back to work not let it get to me but it did and then I keep it to myself for a while like a lot of secret I haven't told Kim Butter thru rest of the week. But then the following week as I came home Kim Butter there as she asked me how was work and I just let it out saying parents called bothering me about not going to Jevone wedding and stuff as she said stop letting them call you at work. She then was mad saying you can't let them mess with you at the job because your family is and when she said that I started to come at her defending them saying they not just have problems and that is still my parents so she was upset saying stop defending and attacking me when I am on only one on your side. I then just went into my room without her closing the door while she was in living room and stayed to myself for a while later came out to eat dinner but she didn't make anything for me and that was our first real couple argument that I don't want to happen again because my parents are the pain in my life that I got to stop covering up or I never get healing. So, the last two days in the week it was a little quiet with Kim Butter she was still mad at me because she didn't want to hear it about my family and I had to make it right so that Friday I got off work and went to gallery venders to get her some flowers bring home. I came in she was there and I just gave it to her saying sorry for letting parents get to me and not listen to you love you as she took them and smiled saying she loves me back and we enjoyed the rest of our night for us turning off the phone answering machine so it just rung on low to do us. Then that Saturday we woke up from a peaceful night to then enjoy another planning for us weekend but then Jevone called after 10am to remind me that I had to have that white best man outfit ready and I told him I will because with just 2 months before my younger brother will be married and I don't want to miss it but did tell him we bought a car. We talked for a while then I had to go spend rest of my time with Kim Butter and we enjoyed our weekend together that I was outside cleaning our car with Kim Butter then hit me saying she wants to learn how to drive and I told her I will teach her but said I not going to yell at her. We did go out downtown toward some more stores as Kim Butter checked out more wedding dresses and I was looking for my best man suit and then finally found one it was nice suit so I tried it on and it fit great as I put what was the minimum down to hold it. It was nice to finally do that for my brother's wedding then we enjoyed rest time weekend and got home chilled that Sunday. Back to work Monday was feeling better and happier because I made things rite with the love of my life and got my suit so did a lot rite and knowing that we will be next. We went to work Friday and it was a quick and fast pace day no problems or phone calls so I was happy leaving out wishing my friends and coworkers a great weekend and ready to get home to my baby to do some preview loving and cuddling that is something we like to do too. She was home and told me her family called talked to them and everybody was fine as she does have a big family and her parents miss her want her to come over because her mom always has something to give her so we end up stopping by over there since we were budgeting for our wedding so we had to slow down on going out a lot. Saturday was here and she had me up ready to go store opens at 10am plus had to go her wedding dress too so we had a lot of running around to do and we enjoyed ourselves and all I know that since she been my fiancée talking and planning and talking that all I do is say yes and just listen like a good fiancée. As we got down there driving instead of taking the bus because it was parking so found the agent and put money down then went to her wedding dress store as I sat in the car not looking and by the time that she came out hour later she was smiling because she finally had an ideal of what dress she wanted and said toward the fall the dresses prices go down. So, we accomplished exactly what we needed to do and then got some lunch headed back home but stop by her family house see parents chilled there for a while as she talked her mouth off the wedding dress to her mom and sister while I chilled with her that father and brother watching tv. It was nice then we left headed back home with her mom good cooked food she gave us and relaxed rest of the weekend with her talking all about the dress that I couldn't even get chance to use the phone and it was cool if she was happy then I was doing my job. Thru the month of May and into June we were saving like for our wedding and honeymoon trip and not spending on us but still did some looking at future things like our wedding rings and her colors for her wedding plus she was deciding who be her maid of honors and she wanted four so I had to come up with 3 grooms and of course Jevone would be my best man just like I am going to be for his wedding too.

So, she was writing and calling people and planning so much that every night we talked about it dinner and before we went to bed so this was not the time to get scared but still I couldn't mess up her happy mood by telling her my parents are not even coming to Jevone wedding and will do the same to ours too so kept my mouth shut. With June here and a month to go before my younger brother gets married I was heading downtown afterwork to pick up my suit to wear before they run out and got back home later to a sleepy fiancée waiting up for me but she had something to tell me saying my parents called so many times it got on her nerves that she turned the answering machine off and pulled the cord phone out not something I wanted to hear. All I know is that I had to call them back though she didn't want me too but I told her I handle it like I always don't so she of course went to bed mad and sent the phone outside of the bedroom so I can talk. And knew this wasn't going to be good but had to stand up to them show Kim Butter she not marrying a punk but a man that will defend her and our future and I not under their control or roof anymore as I still hiding a deep secret that I can't tell her just not yet.

I called my parents back talking to mom telling her we are doing okay but asking why calling so much you know I working as she got mad saying is Kim Butter stopping you again from talking to us. I said no we been busy planning for our wedding and still going to Jevone so she tried to say I against their wishes and I don't respect them as I told her I got to go to bed just don't call so much and love yall hanging up. Knowing she wanted to argue all night I left the phone off the hook so we can sleep in peace and that was that. Thru the rest of the week me and Kim Butter had a leave us alone week and enjoyed our weekend as every weekend we were talking and planning for our wedding on who's going to be in it and what church we going to get married at but she said we must see the pastor who is going to marry us too. This was a lot to take in but also with us already in 2nd week of June my younger brother Jevone getting married next month July 8th we had to get ready for so I had my suit and we went out to get her a nice dress and shoes as shoes for me too. We got a lot of things done as couple and before we knew it was two weeks before the wedding as we were putting each month payments on our trip and Kim Butter decided to go to the church down the street from our apartment and check it out. It was a Preston Church as she meets the pastor and came back telling me that he wants to meet us and talk to us so as usual she didn't waist any time already have the church taken care of that is my baby gets things done. As I was talking to Jevone about being his best man and what time he wants me there giving directions how I can get there as one day that week Wednesday I came home and Kim Butter told me she had picked decided on how many brides maid she wants and who which is 4 so I had to get four men for my groomsmen knowing that I need to get on the ball because I only get one shot at marrying her and better not come up short our special day. Things was coming at us so fast that this was the last week to get ready for Jevone wedding that is this Saturday so I made sure we got in our last shopping this weekend so we do not have to thru this week and we went out that morning going downtown to the stores picked out a nice dress for her and shoes and mines too under our budget then to her wedding dress store for her decided what dress she wanted as they were on sale. So, we headed home but went to her family house to talk to her parents about our wedding plans and her sister being in it so that was a long day but I still enjoyed being of their house. As that day ended with us finally getting home then straight to bed because Sunday I had to try on my suit make sure it fit me and Kim Butter her outfit matches as we relaxed but seeing ourselves as next in line to walk down that aisle that I cannot worry about my family being there or not just trying still to keep peace though Kim Butter see it as a waist of time. Heading toward the work week I had to finish projects for the Fraiction Store Company making up signs but was talking about getting married to Kim Butter to my nice coworkers like Malandy and the guys were happy for me and with not having a that father to talk to it filled the gap okay. During the week I was talking to Jevone about directions and my suit color he was okay with it and we had to leave early because his wedding was at 3pm so we had to travel to Delaware which I never been too but it be worth it see my brother get married. Rest of the week was wonderful week with Friday here I went to get my haircut as Kim Butter got her hair done as well so we were ready for a preview of what we will be experiencing next year. It was the day July 8th my brother's wedding and I was so excited like it was our day that we both woke up early and got ourselves something to eat then got out clothes out as I was calling Jevone talking to him saying we be there and so happy to see my younger brother getting married too. So, of course the subject of mom and dad not coming got him upset but I told him to focus on his beautiful bride as he did then Kim Butter got on phone wish him congratulation and to him soon be bride too so we did our part then went to get ourselves together for later. Then came the call from my parent's mom calling asking me am I going and I said yes somebody must be there for him yall not so she tried to argue with me and my sister talking in the back too was not good she in agreement with this mess too. I couldn't talk to them anymore so I had to shut it down telling mom yall not rite and I don't expect yall to be at mines either but we still going to get married and hung up as Kim Butter was proud of me finally standing up to my parent's evil ways because this is a special day for both families that nobody needs to be mad. As time was flying by fast it was 12:30 pm and we wanted to get an early start not to get lost plus get gas too so as we tried to leave and I was making sure we had everything then closed the door putting the key in top lock but it got stuck in the top lock and I couldn't get it out for a few minutes. As then Kim Butter tried still stuck I tried again as it was 10 mins later and then as I tried to turn the key broke in half with the rest stuck in the door locked it was the strangest things we ever imagine happening of all things on this day it was . I tried to get the rest of it out but couldn't it was deep broke in there with our apartment unlock and we didn't know what to do so for hour trying to see what to do we couldn't leave apartment open like that as it was after 1;00 pm and wedding is 2 hours from now I had to call Jevone and let him know what happened that I know he be upset so as Kim Butter tried to calm me down I called him and told him what happened to the key broke in the door he was upset saying now he have nobody from family coming to wedding and I was so upset for him to me being his best man that he had to go hanging up and I knew that this is exactly what my evil parents wanted. This was but all we could do was just try to find a way to get there but I knew this is not going to happen as it was 2;00 pm and she was upset saying we not going but then we have this Chinese neighbor and she nice so Kim Butter went to talk to her telling her what happen but she didn't speak good English. Trying to tell her what happen took 30 mins more until she finally understood and then she said watch our apartment which was a blessing as we then went on our way as it was already heading toward 3;00 pm start of the wedding while Kim Butter told me calm down don't drive either we don't need to get into accident. So, with her telling me the directions and I already told Jevone I can't make it still wanted to be there for him from my side family so driving where we never been before that by the time we got there the wedding was almost over and we Jevone hugging somebody and it was that father he did come what a shocker as me and Kim Butter walked up to Jevone hugging him and his new wife saying congratulations we sorry we late with the door key breaking off but happy for yall as they went into their limo on their way to the reception that we couldn't go to because we still had to get back to our apartment. It was nice to see Jevone so happy with his wife that I know I not going to let anything my family does stop us from getting married because this is what is meant to be. We headed back to our apartment Kim Butter started thinking about our wedding saying she wants a big wedding like theirs too and I agreed so we need to save more as we got back to the apartment and everything was fine with the Chinese lady did watch out apartment and we thanked her for that too as we just locked the bottom door and waited until Monday to get the apartment guy to fix our door get broken key out. We just relaxed that Sunday as she was talking about how nice my sister- in- law wedding dress look and was now thinking about the colors that she wanted too so that was all thru the day thing but lucky she had girlfriends and her mom, sisters to talk to so I could relax watch some sports on tv. Still, it was a great weekend for the Cylence family my younger brother got married without my parents drama and that what I was happy about me being next. But then how am I going to handle my messy family when it comes my time that hopefully they learn their lesson you can't stop when happiness is put together whether they accept us or not. As I we talked all night about our marriage that she specific about who she wanted there and who she didn't because she had family too that she didn't like either but her immediate family still supported her so that was good. All Kim Butter did was talk about my brother's wedding saying we going to do this instead and it gave her ideal how ours was going to be so I know now that I have a great fiancée that going to make sure everything goes ok for us and us only because we are the ones paying for majority of it with some help from her parents but none from mines and that is the way I like it no you owe me anymore. The week was here back to work and we both woke up just still thinking now about our wedding day that it stayed on

our minds thru the day as we went to work and I got to my job happy
for my brother telling my coworkers what also tried to stop us from
going too with me as the best man was but we still made it there. All
I could think about is that I will make sure you we don't have that
problem again and get that key lock fixed as soon as possible so we
don't have to worry about our stuff but then she wanted to talk about
moving to another apartment because didn't want be here anymore
after the accident. Telling me that she checked out couple of places
and had two that we could afford one in west Philly close to here
then another one on Haverford avenue nice too but cheaper and not
around college students. Thru the next two weeks with my birthday
not far we did have some money saved up and when she wants
something being already an independent woman, she does it as I was
thinking about it but told her it's her decision and I follow wherever
you go. As I didn't want to be here either we decided to call the one
in Haverford and checked it out was nice near transportation but had
this big complex clean and they showed us the one bedroom was
sweet with a balcony and they had swimming pool too with us having
carpet and big living room nice kitchen. After seeing that place and
we had already made decision this is the place for us so we needed to
come up with at least first and last month rent was $1600 so we had
most of it just needed another two more week with them saying we
can move in the beginning of August. We were so happy to be away
from Peppers City area as it was time to move so with us saving that
we needed to do this or we regret it. So then with two weeks before
my birthday I was still feeling the pressure of getting married as I
didn't think I was getting anything for my birthday with us saving
for the wedding and moving too so I didn't mention it just prayed for
us to continue enjoy our lives together. Thru that week we put the
money aside needed to move but then got messeges from my messy
parents of why we were there but I tried to ignore them with Kim
Butter erasing them so I don't hear them when I came home from
work but the problem still was that they call my job because I had
given them the work#. One day with it July and couple weeks before
my birthday my mom called the job in the morning asking to talk to

me so I had to take the call and she just came out saying why haven't I returned her calls is Kim Butter already making you distant from us and that if I keep it up nobody will be there so I had to tell her sorry and that I will talk to them when I get off work didn't want my coworkers knowing my problems. But later that day I did talk to my parents telling them we just wanted to be there for Jevone since you said not going but we didn't know that dad would be there as I was still trying to keep peace with my parents because I wanted them to be there at my wedding I done for them so I just said love yall got to go and hung up knowing this is not over. We were doing everything we could to budget and saving money left and right for the wedding and then ready to move into the apartment too as it was important for us for find a church to get married in that she was going to take care of that but I was making sure my tuxedo was available at reasonable price too then who would be my best man Jevone as her second oldest sister was her brides maid. Then we were talking about how many on both sides and Kim Butter only wanted 4 bridesmaids so I had to have four groomsmen including best man with my oldest brother Terance do not really talk to so I went to work with my birthday July a week away asking my two coworkers Lanley and Sufon if they would be my groomsmen in my wedding next year and they said sure as I was so happy to have them two married men. So, then I felt happy to have them two wanting be in my wedding now I must get two more men so I asked Jevone then Roney my soon to be brother- in- law. Next week my birthday wondering what Kim Butter has planned for me since it be special with us next year getting married too but hope she do not spend a lot we need all our money to save with what type of wedding she wants to have and her family not able to really help us so we on our own but know God will help. Friday I was trying to get out office heading home little tired and feeling good I did not get any phone calls from my messy parents even at the job like they usually bother me so I know that it will not be long before they will bother me just a matter of time. I left out heading home knowing Kim Butter was always beating me home anyway just be glad to see her miss my baby so that I was falling asleep on trolley tired want to sleep that I almost missed my stop though it was crowded on there too but I did get a seat because walking to Marred street where the trolleys just come up. By time I got home it was after 5:30pm I did get there with Kim Butter open the door for me I ringing the doorbell as she ask me how was my day and I just said it was good ready for whatever she made for dinner just wanted to rest in her arms. So, then it was still a lot on me because we were still trying to save for our honeymoon in Disney even the new apartment end of this month so I was not asking for nothing for birthday but to be with her and not talk to nobody or my parents either because know they going to call me try to ruin my birthday. As I went to work that day was nothing unusual but I did remind my coworkers that couple days is my birthday so they were happy for me as I be turning 25yrs old and happier than I been in years with a wonderful fiancée too helps a whole lot. I felt like I now not scared anymore that the real me is starting to come out and protect what I been going thru to get here no matter who not happy for me because they were controlling my joy anyway but not no more. And that is how I was feeling thru that week not even thinking about how many times my parents were still calling my job bothering me trying to make me lose my job then even at home leaving nasty messeges like why haven't you called us we still your family like really when was that when yall was abusing me. But I know it's because I was the last one to escape like my brothers did while they were thinking I be on their side of them leaving but I was not going to stay there and start another abuse control attack on my life.

21

HIDDEN A NEW BEGINNING

Trying to stay focus on the good stuff then it was that day with tomorrow my birthday I came home to wife so happy as she was letting me know we are going out and she has a surprise for me too which I wasn't expecting with us trying to move and save but with her budgeting anything is possible. That night was peaceful because we took the phone off the hook so we couldn't be disturbed but enjoy each other without interruptions and we were putting stuff in boxes because with us finding the apartment we were trying to move rite after my birthday so we be in a peaceful place. Thru next couple days it was business as usual I was going to work and Kim Butter as well enjoying her job working downtown now at new company was good for her because she was applying for this a long time and just happen that Thursday got the job as I was so happy for my future wife. All I know that god was keeping us together despite how her family felt and knew how they are love couldn't break us up not this time so we continued to save and pack up that I almost forgot what day it was from working so hard that it was my birthday as I still had to go to work needed the money. What made it still a great morning waking up to my future as she hugged and kissed me

147

wishing me happy birthday and had a card for me that I loved it then said after work we going out as I said okay that be great and told her I love her then got ready to go to work and it was wonderful day for me that not even my messy parents called me that morning bless my heart. While at work my coworkers were very nice as I told them it's my birthday and they wished me a great one then my closet friends had a card for me and balloons was nice to see they really liked me and not using me like my family done. Almost an perfect day that I didn't even care about all the signs and work I had to do but still enjoying my day until that call came in and I knew it was coming my parents calling me in a attitude telling me why didn't you answer your phone this morning wanted to wish you happy birthday but I told them I at work that's why as that dad got on saying don't talk to your mother like that we still your family like I need them to remind me that!! So, I tried to keep the conversation short and not be talking all loud as my coworkers were hearing their voices on phone telling them can yall just say it thanks for calling and I have to get back to work as mom got back on phone saying fine but don't expect anything okay so I just still saying after all I been thru love yall and hung up trying to get my joy back after they did try to take it. The day almost over and people from other departments wishing me happy birthday I felt like I was really a person that somebody appreciate that I never felt in a long time being trapped in that prison that my parents kept us from experiencing living life. The day was over and I left out running couldn't wait to see Kim Butter so we can go out and enjoy my birthday with her that I almost forgot to clock out just was so happy to celebrate this day not around my parents abuse again. Got home rite behind her and she kissed me and we hugged then she gave me a nice gift of nice shirt that she bought it was great because I had this problem of my clothes colors just always matching almost too much like a nerd that with her flavor trying to bring me out of that dull shell. So we got dress and she had plans to take me out but still her family did call me to wish me happy birthday and that was nice to hear normal people not that you owe us we still your parents story.. I thanked them too because its Kim Butter parents that bless me to have a women that still wanted to share her life with me and my mess that makes this birthday nothing I could have ever imagined. With it getting later we got car then it was on we went to eat dinner and movies what a night and came home to some loving each other that she was the gift I always wanted and been waiting for to rescue me that she did do. The next day we both didn't wake up until couple hours later being Saturday still had to pack up because next week would be our last time living here since we did tell the landlord that we like move in by August 1st but I still was enjoying my birthday weekend with Kim Butter as we was cleaning up and stuff pretty much thru the day then going store for empty boxes and trash bags because with working next week it be hard to do all of this. And while things was going great as she always talking to either her family or girlfriend as the phone was free in came that terrible call from my parents of course my mom all loud on the answering machine saying pick up I know your there why what you doing and is she keeping you from talking to your family just . So, before Kim Butter could hear it I lowered the volume so it wouldn't make her mad as we continued to clean but then that didn't stop them as they kept calling and calling back because that is how disrespectful they are but with everything from that dad that I am still keeping secret to myself you think he worry about upsetting me and stop mom but now I know have to soon put stop to this just not today. It was still upsetting Kim Butter so what she did was just disconnected the phone so it was completely off and stop all that drama then saying what is wrong with your family I can't believe they are your parents as I had to take that what she was saying is truth but then don't talk about them like that okay and walked away to clean. As they always do have us arguing now we mad at each other ruining our good time is what they do because if they are not happy they will make sure we not either including Jevone that is enjoying his honeymoon with his new wife too. For a few hours all we did was just clean and box for a while then we rested but she was in the bedroom got the phone back on and was talking either her mom or girlfriends ear off about my family that I hope it didn't push her to second guess marrying me because that would just break my heart forever. With that going on for a while and into the evening that by time I did get chance to talk to her was ask what was for dinner and she gave me a look like you must be ask me anything that I just sat down watch tv again knowing that look meant nothing. Eventually she did fix me dinner but left it in the kitchen as she went to her room to eat and talk more about me that when it was time go to bed as I turned tv off and went bed with her luckily as I said sorry to her then just looked at me saying your family need prayer and Jesus but still kiss me as we made peace together and not separated. We still made up and enjoyed the rest of our weekend together then heading back to work that week thankful this is our last week in this apartment to a better place where we can enjoy our lives together next year as a married couple. Meanwhile back at work things were say and good with us still enjoying nice times together with my coworkers but the one I really cool with was Malandy as she always asked me are we ready still get married and I said yes but my family getting on my nerves and she laugh saying don't let them stop you which was good to hear from her though she isn't. Just that type of friendship kept me focus on knowing our happiness is going to change a whole lot of stuff from what we can't be around anymore because we pleasing us not our families this is our time to enjoy the love we have for each other whether they like it or not. Still with my parents calling me at home and the job I did the best I could ignoring them while Alfonso and Malandy took the messeges for me as many times they called still didn't stop looking out for me was good to know that I would go on break sometimes by myself to think and talk or with Lanley and his friend with both men being married they telling me stay focus your almost there helped a lot. The days were counting down and with both of us getting paid on the same week we had to go that Thursday and rented a Handler truck to move our furniture that weekend and be in the apartment Monday August 1st so we couldn't waist anytime. Kim Butter had asked her that father and brother to help us move which was great ideal because I didn't have anyone to ask with Jevone on his honeymoon too. By the time we knew it was Friday and we went to pick up her brother and that father rented the Handler Truck then started to put stuff in it that night to get ahead started into the morning me and Kim Butter was going over to the new Daley Apartment and pay for it then get our keys to move in over the weekend be in there by Monday. So, by time we had finish putting as much as we could the major stuff with that slim small steps we all was tired as Kim Butter brother and dad was tired taking them home so they be able again to help us move next day and then got back falling out in the bedroom clothes on and all. Saturday we was ready to start at new location that she got me up with same clothes on making some type of breakfast with tea because I like tea then we headed out to Daley Apartment and met the landlord talked about how much a month then that we be there for 2yrs just to start paid for it then celebrated our new apartment checking it out. It was so nice that we had more space then, we thought with a nice big dining room, and a dishwasher with a nice kitchen, then a little deck sliding door and cream carpet with air conditioner plus a nice big bedroom window view of the swimming pool was all that too. Nice bathroom too that I almost forgot that we had to leave to get out stuff so eventually after hour we did leave so happy heading to her family house to get her brother and dad to help us move was a blessing to me. So, with her brother driving and most of the stuff in the truck already we got back heading to our new location and it wasn't far just up not far from Atlas Avenue plus bus transportation to Upper street too so that was a great thing to know as we got there and just started unloading things as the apartment had plenty of parking spots with it so big too and elevators as well. With us needing cards to get it that made us feel better with that type of security as well as we took the heavy stuff upstairs where the apartment was on the 2nd floor good thing as we had got the big stuff up there and then beds and mattress then the rest of the furniture that by then my soon to be brother-in-law was tired but we still getting it done also. Before we finished going back and forth took us 3 trips, we had taken everything out of that apartment that all we had to do that Sunday was clean the rest of it and that was the plan all along so we chilling in our new apartment was so wonderful that all we did was looking around like little kids but still had to take the A-Hall truck back plus Kim Butter dad and brother home they were tired but we did treat them to something eat and drink. then headed back to apartment sleeping in our new bedroom for a while and that was a feeling we been waiting to do since the incident and now enjoying brand new place with it so clean and up to date that it was like we living in a palace and my parents don't even know. Now with everything us settled in our apartment and Kim Butter already had our number changed over because she took care of stuff like that including our address at the post office so everything was done quickly as we was getting familiar with the place that we had multiple entrances for us with your card and parking was free too. As it was still nice out the apartment had air conditioning and a washer and dryer on each floor though we had to pay but no need go outside was good to know. I never thought we be in such a great place and planning a wedding too that I know god must be on our side so while I was resting in the bed still Kim Butter was wiping off the kitchen down guess that is something her mom tells her when move into a new place plus we didn't have to buy a refrigerator they provided that so the old one stayed there and that was fine with us though she was wiping that out too. By time she was done she had the bathroom wiped down too with bleach and pine soil to make it smell better plus she told me when you move into a new place always wiped down things so you give it that new fresh scent and I not about to tell her she wrong either. What a way to enjoy the rest of this year at new place and a beautiful fiancée I must be dreaming that I had to pinch myself make sure I was wide awake for this. Now my messy parents didn't know where I live at or home# makes it even more sweet except that now they be trying to embarrass me at work even more so I have to shut that down because this is not the time to get scared because one of these days I going to have to standup to them and that day is coming. What a great time we were having in our new apartment that we didn't go anywhere for those next two day just relaxed and moved furniture around then with the phone just not on yet Kim Butter went to pay phone to call her parents telling her how nice it is plus her dad and brother talked about it too. This must be again a dream because for all this to come out of everything that I been thru with being abused physically and verbal now to be a year away from being a married man like Jevone and a nice place to live with a car god is good. And all that time he still was there hearing my cries and hurts, pains to let me know God still loves me while I still keeping things secret from Kim Butter God made this happen and I so happy I don't want it to end. Then we went back to work together as I would take her to job then I take care someplace at job and park it down there sometimes too so then I don't have to catch the bus but didn't mind. Work was good as then next couple of weeks in apartment we started to see our neighbors and the kind of people living in there was okay with a mixture of races but also a lot of women with kids and stuff so it was something. Then with us in the middle of August already we were still budgeting even more because this place wasn't cheap but costing little more that I didn't know how we afford it but my fiancée is a very independent woman making it on her own before we met so I know she can pull this wedding off too. Knowing then that my family been calling my job saying why my phone# changed and all I could do was say I will give them the new phone# soon but please don't call my job so much or I get in trouble and as I said that to that dad since he was home not working only mom. I should have been letting him have it saying I still keeping your secret just don't know why but trying to keep the peace between Kim Butter and my family so they still come to our wedding. Then we were sending money to our trip to Disney World that Kim Butter was still had us saving even though we just moved in here but what she wanted is what I had to do for her so I was then trying to work overtime at the job like a half hour here and they sometimes let me do it because we needed it especially I was paying for her wedding dress too then also we had to find a location to have the reception too but I let that up to her. So, things were going okay until we had to get our phone on and did giving her family the phone# but not mines because didn't want them bothering us for a while though I could call them just my phone# came up private was good thing. One day over the weekend while me and Kim Butter was relaxing we decided to go into the swimming pool because it was so nice and we saw people out there having fun but I can't swim and neither could she still we went anyway. It was nice but crowded with black people and kids but we went and just got our feet wet as everybody was looking at us new to the complex but we say hi some said it back while others just looked. I just chilled with Kim Butter and it was fun then she told me it's time to go in and we did so as going in she told me some women were looking at me but I didn't notice still she said if they keep doing that she was going to shut it down and I just smiled saying she really happy with me and I never felt so much joy that we did some loving each other thru that weekend like we were already married. I will do the best that I can to protect what god put into my life and try not to let nothing or family take this away from us we deserve this. Still, we enjoyed our time for us and it was wonderful that I almost didn't want to leave the apartment but of course we still had to go to work just how clean and modern it was with a dish washer as much as Kim Butter don't do dishes and I do I might[1] use that. So that was most of our weekends still budgeting not going out as much only to movie and that is it not too much hanging out with friends had to calm that down trying to save and still pay our bills too. While heading back to work was cool as people were asking me are we planning and saving as I said yes and that was cool my coworkers cared plus it was a little peace of mind with me in control of talking to my parents since we both still was undecided when to give my family our new phone#. But still they found ways to still bother me at work a bit as last time I told them I need this job stop calling so much I will call you and that just mad that dad and mom even more mad at me more like Kim Butter was controlling me they say but I just didn't want her and my family mad at me so I was without her knowing it talking to them on break and afterwork at payphone being nice to them and apologizing saying we just stress about saving and getting married. Now came couple weeks where they only called like twice out week but still bothered me little as I was just trying to get thru month of August going by fast with a lot of work at the job of merchandise discounted down so making a lot of signs was a must project. All that work and overtime did help my wallet a lot because I had no other way of making extra money and I wasn't about to any part-time work wanted to spend time with my baby. Working so much and not doing too much partying or spending was good because we were getting a lot of rest and time alone but still, she had her girlfriends calling her and parents too while mines still didn't have our phone# but I had to keep in touch by calling them though it still made my parents mad. With August flying by I did remember this month was Terance birthday but know he somewhere hopefully enjoying it while not speaking to any of us and all I could do was hope he was safe and okay that's it. Then Kim Butter was telling me at home from work one day that the total for our trip is close to $2000 and we still got time to pay it off so I still wanted to do it just hope maybe with our taxes that help out too because you only get married once and this be my first and last time she is the love of my life. Then things at work started to change where they had us in training for some new way to do our signs and so I was excited plus a new copy machine now too so we all had to learn how to use it and that was okay with me hopefully more money. So, this happen for the next couple of weeks training thru September that I was coming home so tired I go straight to bed then later at night wake up in late evening eating and watching tv because I couldn't sleep from having bad dreams about that dad touching me. It was still affecting me little as the next night I went to bed but again it happened and Kim Butter get woken up asking am I okay I just said had bad dream about my family so she just held me saying it's okay because couldn't even talk about it just crying little only to stay up rest night. This continued thru the rest of the weeks into the weekend that I would start staying up late for a while not wanting to go to bed as Kim Butter would try to watch tv with me but then headed to bed leaving me up rest night to myself because I just couldn't come out say why is this happening not now with us soon to be married too. Going to work little tired and almost falling asleep at the desk that some of my coworkers asking am I okay all I could say was yeah lying don't want them saying stuff like I getting nervous about marriage when that's not it. For the next couple weeks almost two to 3 times out week I use trying to watch sports like basketball or baseball reason why I stay up late and it was all I could say so Kim Butter don't get worried. With me still not sleeping well it started to affect how I was acting and reacting toward Kim Butter that thru the month of September I did call my brother Jevone to wish him happy birthday as he was still enjoying just getting married and it was late in the evening but Kim Butter was trying to get me to go to bed and I was giving he hard time. Then I was getting into wanting to argue with her saying like I can stay up I not no kid and don't bother me things like that as she was getting upset like I didn't want to be around her but that wasn't it just didn't want to go to sleep as this was not good way to head toward marriage arguing. Things were little after that because she started to talk about this with her parents worried that we weren't going to make it so as I was trying to ignore her plea to not be scared and sleep as summer was over with me just working and saving money that was all me and Kim Butter did. Now she wanted to go she her parents one weekend to make sure they okay and talk to her sister and brother that was a setup to have me talk to her dad and ask me am I okay like do I still want to get married to his daughter and is there something I need to talk to him about he and her brother are here for me. That was nice because I did feel like I don't know how long I can keep all this inside and not tell Kim Butter but I had to didn't want her to leave me either and that would break my heart then my parents would win and I be back in that abuse and hurt place again and I made it this far don't want go back there. As we had a good time and left I never felt a family caring for me instead of using me before like Kim Butter family done for me that I wish they were my real family but all I can do now is just continue to hope mines get the wakeup call to stop hurting each other it stops your happiness. Going home that night I was seeing why Kim Butter is such a strong woman with family like that still keeping their joy not worrying what they don't have just still moving forward that is why I have to not mess up what been put in front of me a beautiful strong woman and future partner that wants to be with me and all my secrets that she does have an ideal I been thru something and loves me anyway. Can't help but to not let that make me open up because I know I can keep it together and we get married if I don't then it will just let my family saying I made a mistake rushing to get away and do what Jevone did but this is me taking control my life with my parents still having hold of me and that's hard to break that chain too. As we went to bed because it was getting late and with tomorrow back to work Kim Butter was still asking me come to bed with her don't watch late tv but all I could do was not argue just say okay. For the first time in a while, I just lay down closed my eyes with her holding me saying she loves me it going to be okay and that was all I needed to hear slept like a baby with peace not scared just glad she was holding me praying saying When Two Come Together We Touch and Agree To Take Out 10,000 Attacks Against Us Amen and I went to sleep knowing the attacks will stop. The next day woke up not in the middle of the night but morning and was so happy to see that god did protect me last night from the bad dreams all because my fiancée prayers that I never had anybody praying for me like she did now I know it's going to be a fight for us to make it and can't fall down not now. We went to work I kissed her saying I love you and glad you want to still marry me with my mess as we started to catch the trolley this time because gas and parking was too high for us to pay so that was nice us catching trolley together and she get off at Hightenstreet while I went to Wittin street and I felt so stronger not weak that I know this is what I want for me. And work was even good too with us learning new system I was catching on and doing my job great plus my coworkers were okay as now I see that something was trying to keep me unhappy from seeing what some people like to be getting married to someone that loves them too as Malandy wasn't but she still was happy for me. It helped me get thru staying that way each day and for the next couple of weeks I was focus not letting my parents though they were calling me at job harassing me saying I need to come see them and stuff like I still live there but I did my best. Then that dad called me one Wednesday in September saying he been sick and mom too that I need to not forget they my parents and check up on us making me feel bad as I said okay sorry I will and then asking me come up there so I had to and then keep it a secret from Kim Butter what they said. It was something I did because I needed her to still understand that is my parents no matter how they acting I got to see them so I had went home to her and told her they were sick and I need to see them as she was upset but said fine just don't let them make you feel bad because you know they don't like me as I just said okay. With work going good I was just trying to finish strong week as Friday was here and that evening went to go see my parents afterwork because she didn't to see them plus our weekends for us too much we trying to do with still having to go pay her wedding dress and our honeymoon too that was our time together. I was leaving that dad still hugged telling me he loves me and mommy too then I hugged and kissed Kevin and tried to hug Bernadette but she was resentful as I went to mom but she was like no I got bad cold don't want you fiancée getting my cold bye so I just left out saying I come see yall again okay it won't be a problem and left out finally with relief but still frustrated what they said about me and Kim Butter family too but serve them rite I had to go outside to really get love from another family not out to hurt or abuse me just like my brothers left too and so will Bernadette. Getting out there was such a relief almost couldn't breathe that I was about to cry but was keeping it inside and add it to the rest of stuff until one day I going to explode just not at Kim Butter but to people that put it in me and never thought about the repercussions. I was driving a little fast too wanted to get out of New Jersey but careful of the cops out here give me a ticket and don't care so kept it cool and was almost home heading to Philly where it's safe and with my fiancée just can't let her know what they said or she will flip out must let her know everything's okay they fine nothing else she needs to hear because she knows they said something smart anyway. I got home and she was still up waiting for me said I was worried are you okay I said yeah just tired long ride but they okay mom was sick and that dad lot of pain too but I got them medicine and missed Kevin and Bernadette so then we just went to bed didn't want to talk about them anymore as she knows I hiding something from her but that is to protect her and our lives together. Thru that night I was then again having problem sleeping upset and that is what they do to me barely going back to sleep as Kim Butter knew it that thru the next day Saturday I was still in the bed that morning not even getting up while she was up fixing breakfast and watching tv I just wanted to be left alone in bedroom talking to myself parents after everything I been thru and they telling me off when I should be the one cussing them out and now, I was hurting all over again but got to keep it together can't be a weak man with a strong woman. By time I got up it was after 11 am because cartoons were still on which is something I still watch little kid in me and Kim Butter does too that's another thing we have in common too so I just said hi as she kissed me hugging me saying am I okay just said yeah lying but she still asked what did my family say because I know they said something smart but I just said nothing too sick and I just took care of them. Had to keep it short don't want to talk about anymore but she knows me and that I was hiding something still in my face saying we about to be married can't hold things inside as a secret from me then I said I okay they still the same but I was fine okay and left it at that heading into kitchen to eat as she knew I was getting mad and left me alone was the best thing to do don't want to argue already we haven't been in new place a month yet. The rest of the weekend I was not talking that much just to myself with Kim Butter always likes to talk things out I don't rather keep it inside still not sure she be able to handle my past with us still not married yet. She did go she her parents that Sunday while I relaxed watching tv and sports that was my escape from the present so I don't think about exploding at her when it's not her fault what I been thru that I think about needing to talk to a doctor about everything that dad did to me and mom too so I can get help and not hurt myself or our marriage. So later that Sunday she got some air and time with her caring family asked me was I okay and I said yes and sorry telling her love you it's not you just want things to go good for us to be married and enjoy our honeymoon but she just said stop worrying it will work out okay and we spent rest of the night enjoying each other in the love that brought us together. That time with Kim Butter help me to get thru going to work that whole week and nobody can make me forget things like she does because I see she praying woman that know god but I don't talk to him like I should for help and need to because with me soon to be her husband can't punk out but standup to my parents and let them know this is my family and love us or leave us alone. So, going back to work was good for me being around my funny coworkers too motivated me to see that I can do this with us both working so hard we were getting home so late that by time it was time to eat dinner it was then bedtime but she still would have time to talk to her girlfriends and then her family too that never going to stop. Trying to work and save for our marriage was tiresome that I didn't talk to my brother Jevone that much either with him still newly married but that was okay as long as he was happy and not letting our parents upset him and his new wife was the key. I was thinking about doing something like letting my parents have our house # but had to ask Kim Butter instead of lying to her which I still doing about other things to ask her on a day where we both can talk about it like the weekend. So as the days then turned to weeks then months and not asking her but I was still getting harassed at work by them so much it got on my upsetting that one day during week of October and heading toward Halloween with coworkers talking my parents called me again at work and it was that dad asking why I don't love them anymore like they don't exist as I was trying to do my work telling him I can't talk rite now. He still wouldn't hang up saying what if we have emergency with Kevin seizure or his bad back how can we reach you so as I was trying to not let my coworkers Malandy see me upset I had to just say okay get him off the phone but telling him I call him give it to them later and then apologizing sorry love yall. See they still have a hold on me making feel guilty every time like I abandoned them when I had to escape or I wanted to hurt that dad all I could do was go to the bathroom and cry a little how much this is still stressing me out and don't want to lose my job too. So, with that happening went home from work to Kim Butter asking me how was my day and I just let it out that my parents keep calling the job mad that they can't get in contact with me for emergency that could jeopardize my job. Then I said can we just let them have our phone number and keep the peace by just speaking to them once a month. She was upset with them calling my job but knew I still have to talk to them deciding over the weekend knowing she is mad at me but sick of them. I just hope and pray that god will change her mind to still let me talk to my parents though they are but just stop them from harassing me. Then keep them in a quiet, nice communication because whether she likes them or not they still be at our weddin hopefully and not have an attitude like they did at Jevone wedding. I just left it alone and try not to take my family issues out on her but like she told me before pray for them not just say it but do it too for myself as well. I do need to pray more from snapping or losing it because want us to make it and be married. It had me even quiet to myself for those couple days at work that my coworkers thought I was sick or having second thoughts about marriage as Lanley would talk to me since he been married and his buddy too as we go on break together thru the gallery I just said I okay trying keep the peace between my family and hers then Sufon started to laugh like really that is normal wait until yall married so I just laughed with them and it was what I needed. Heading back to work finish the day okay with no calls from them what a relief like I thought the phone was broke or something or I was then hoping nothing is wrong because I do have their # that I was thinking about calling but didn't want to keep and enjoy this peaceful time as it was time to leave as it was Friday night and all I wanted to do was get some sleep with all that watching tv every night staying up. When we get paid weekly, I wanted some pizza as Kim Butter wasn't cooking tonight but we relaxed in each other arms and talk about our wedding plans gotten away from with all the negativity around us that we need this time. Coming home so quick just happy to see her buzzing me in because that was the type of alarm they had at this apartment nobody just walking in on us was good thing as I took that elevator and got to 2nd floor as she open door I just kissed her like never before closing the door behind me telling her I love her you're the best thing ever to happen to me and we went out to dinner laughing and having fun that was a great way start a nice weekend off. Waking up next day Saturday to a beautiful Fiancee by my side I didn't want to move and we just chilled there in bed with sun coming thru our bedroom weather changing cold out and Halloween weekend glad we didn't live place kids could bother us either. So, we just chilled that weekend later that day I asked her that question if my parents could have our home# then she just looked at me like she seen a ghost saying I let you know before today is over okay because I know you want to talk to them and not behind my back anymore as I agreed but don't know for how long. With her wanting to go downtown and pay on her wedding address plus there were some adjustments she wanted to make and also pay on our honeymoon trip too this was always our only time together as we got bundled up with it winter time now and October about to be over this week November is here and Thanksgiving month which I know will be another issue. Going to put more money to pay off her wedding dress was so exciting to me but I couldn't see it otherwise that is bad luck from what her mom told her so I would stand outside of downtown store where she be in there a while because I she wanted no issues. By time she was done a hour had passed but it was cool as we then went to get something eat and then put money on our honeymoon trip it was almost at half that's how much we want this to happen plus she had made phone call to a nice reception place south philly that we also had to pay for. I am so glad I have a fiancée like Kim Butter that was on top of everything that all I had to do was show up because with everything we both are going thru she should be the one about to explode but that is why she is the youngest one only in family that is getting married. Getting back home we didn't waist this day did what we had to do and chilled later that day but still had some unfinished business with my parents that at dinner while eating I asked did she decide if it's okay my parents though they can have our home# for emergency just in case. Kim Butter said okay but if they start calling twenty times and get on my nerves I going to change our number so, I was happy and kissed her doing anything she wanted me to do wash dishes whatever because for my fiancée to meet me halfway like that she really does love me no matter what comes at us. Times likes this make me see that I almost miss my chance to have this beautiful woman as my wife with the first time my parents tried to break us up at her first apartment but I thank God that she still listens to her heart and not to other people because my love for her keeps me sane. We continued to then focus on working toward saving and paying off our wedding event as work was getting harder with stores of need of signs at my job with Thanksgiving just around the corner so we were working my body off. My job was getting calls of more updated signs needed that sometimes I didn't even take lunch but ate at desk because I had a stake of sign forms to enter in system and was quick in typing too was my advantage. Working at this job was nothing but my joy as I still keep my relationship with my coworkers great as I never really had any friends at work or outside always hiding but hopefully that change. This Thursday was Thanksgiving I was still worried because had to let my family know our phone# so knowing they can bother us like they done at my job except that needs to stop now but at least Kim Butter agreed to it not knowing what else they could do to upset us is a chance we taking. With Kim Butter not a driver we still started early going shopping for thanksgiving dinner for us that she wanted to cook for us together but if I know her, she still wants to see her parents get some of their old fashion cooking. I was hoping we still could go see my parents thought it be like a suicide trip but during that week on Tuesday asked her could we go see my family as she was hesitant but said fine go see mines first chill with them and later go over your family that was the plan and I kissed her thankful she giving them a chance but a little one at that. Before we knew it was a day before Thanksgiving and I had done all my signs for that holiday off leaving out wishing all my coworkers happy one. As I was ready to get out of there so tired like I been running on empty, but of course before I left get a phone call from my parents asking what time we coming over to see them and just said yes but I tired leaving out I will call yall before we come by. I know they still but if us coming over there bring them to calm down that would be great because we need some peace and I know Jevone might be there too with his newly wife Jeanette so I like to see her as well. When I got home and fell out just laid out on the couch didn't care what was on tv glad to have day off then she had put the turkey in the oven to cook and hopefully she knows what she doing because I didn't know really but wasn't about to interfere and went to bed not even waking up in the middle of night no bad dreams was good thing. Next day was Thanksgiving it a little later in the morning but glad I was off as we chilled for a while as she was already talking to her parents about coming over then having to see my parent's rite there in front of me too. It was okay then later we were eating early and the turkey was I guess done that she said time to eat and I got dress as she was looking beautiful as usual with mashed potatoes and stuffing knowing she could cook to a man stomach. Things were good and she said okay time to pray and it was nice prayer then she took the turkey out it was good that I never had any woman cook for me was happy she my fiancée as we relaxed then later time to go over her parent's house because they did call us too. Dinner was wonderful I was in so happy that I didn't want go anywhere after eating that food but we had to go see her family then mines so we got out there with it still after 5pm went over her family house. Her mom and family saying Happy Thanksgiving and had some food already on plate for us to eat but I didn't know if I had room for me still ate it and we relaxed watching sports on tv football games with her brother and dad all her sister and nephews over their nice family. Still, her father asked about my family how they doing which is unusual with how they know them to be it was respectful telling them we going to see them tonight as he said tell them I said hi so with that we chilled a while then it was time to go and I didn't want to keep her out late still having to go to work the next day for both of us. I had kissed her mom and hug her sisters and brother, dad saying thanks for food then hurrying up to my parent's house hoping she not too tired to deal with them but she said she is fine just will not take no smart mouth story. from them on she let them have it and I know she meant that too. It took us a hour to get over there even with light traffic that I was still trying to get ready but was okay as we got there and it was such a strange feeling over me because I haven't been here in a long time so I got little nervous but Kim Butter told me you are going to be fine. We rung doorbell and that dad answered the door saying hey how you hugging me and Kim Butter happy Thanksgiving as we came in talk then mom came down and also Jevone and his wife was here nice to see because I didn't want to be by ourselves. We all hugged each other real or not but I missed my brother and Kevin, Bernadette too though she had her rebellious look at me like who you but we still relaxed as I asked Jevone how was their honeymoon and he said still enjoying it. Things were quiet for a while but mom had brought out Thanksgiving turkey platter for us all eat and all I could do was have it to go with that dad having movies for us to watch like he been a great that father and mom too. Still quiet with movie we watching but then spent longer than we thought over there that it was going on 9 pm and my parents of course had to ask Kim Butter is she nervous getting married to me and will we be ready. All I know she just said yeah, we be fine with my mother helping me then it was so quiet you hear down the street as that dad ask how her parents are doing over there but she said they fine we just left them first then I knew it was time to leave because didn't want to leave on a bad note but good terms. We were leaving out they still hug Kim Butter and we hugged Jevone and his new wife too then I kiss Kevin and hugged Bernadette too knowing things will change anyway but at least we trying with Terance didn't even come and I know that he still was mad at them kicking him out so we can't hide the truth will come out but in meantime just want peace. So, we thank my parents for the food to go and then it was time to leave as Jevone and his wife left too but our talk home was something that Kim Butter let me know my family is and controlling still and tried to act like they concern for her parents. I was just listening not about to get her more upset as she was trying not to be but still told her they trying and still my parents as she saw I still defending them after what they done to me because if she only knew the rest it would blow her mind. Had to let her talk it out and only say yeah your rite didn't need us arguing because that is what they wanted to happen anyway and then they win but can't let that happen we still getting married and nothing will stop that except us. By time got home it was late and we just went to bed with tomorrow just do nothing and relax but of course Kim Butter wanted to talk more about my parents as I got upset said okay can we stop talking about them it's over let's go to bed and she saw that as I was getting mad which she was rite. I just wanted to end it then she turned her back on me going to sleep knowing now I the bad guy and but it's my parent's fault so she knew they never change but I need to. Sunday was a don't talk to me day Kim Butter was in her mood that she still was mad about yesterday and was on the phone with anybody she could talk to including her mom and girlfriends saying little things about how she felt funny at my parent's house. Then while I was listening, I got little mad saying Kim stop talking about my family that is still my family and then she looked at me laughing okay sorry but didn't take me seriously still talking but closed the door room. I knew this is going to go on even after we get married so need to just handle her rite or it could be a problem for us because I don't know why I still defending them after all I been thru but just trying keep peace though they ones attacking us. That weekend was nothing talk about stayed away from her chilled in front of the tv as she was quiet but still at least we slept in the same bed didn't change and it helped because it was that back to work mode still have a wedding to make it to. Work was so much better with everybody talking about how great their Thanksgiving was as I just said it was okay with both families and left it at that busy working and focus with 8mos to go before we do this in September so the next couple weeks heading into December Christmas not far away and I still had to give my baby something. Between paying off our honeymoon, her dress and stuff couldn't wait for income tax time to really put more money on things as our rent was $700 too it made it even more difficult but with a fiancée that can budget anything is possible. After seeing my parents made them leave us alone for a while though mom had called us during the week at the apartment to say she had a good time with us and hope to see us again for

Christmas as I was like okay then spoke to Kim Butter too and she said some things trying be nice then hung up knowing that it only last for a month but we take it. I still was trying stop her from talking bad about my family but she was too tired and went bed early letting me know please don't stay up too long because this wanting to cuddle is her thing now so I better not mess that up or I will miss our romance on our wedding night.

Thru the next couple weeks working hard with holiday signs needed and discount numbered signs too there was no room for error because this was our month to win customers and compete in the marketplace so I was typing up sometimes 75 charts a day and had no time for drama but to then go home rest my fingers and eyes and finish the job. I felt like I was important to them and was thinking to myself stop getting upset don't go back at the pain of that little scared boy because I can't be there when I marry my future wife but a man that will take control of his destiny to keep happiness for my life. It helped me little but I still was cutting Kim Butter off when she would ask me secret questions about my past and stuff that I still would get mad saying don't want to talk about it okay that happened over the weekend because she talked about her childhood was rough as an active child. All I could do was listen and say okay that's nice then want to leave go watch tv because I had nothing to give her it all was bad and hurtful that I know me and my brothers are messed up a little but hiding it well otherwise Jevone wouldn't be married and I sure know nobody like Kim Butter want marry me either. I got home to my her and she was so happy to see me telling me she went to get my Christmas gift and do I have hers as I said yes but hope you like it then we kissed and secretly were wrapping up our gifts then chilled as she was trying to get me to tell her something what I bought but my lips were sealed unless she tried to open them by coming at my weakness which is her. By that time, it was getting late and I wanted to be rested up for us to have a bless and peaceful Christmas as our new place but knowing her family and mines will be calling to see us as she had bought her family niece and nephew some toys as well always thinking about her family that she even bought my little brother and sister toys too. And I can never doubt that this is the woman that god bless for my future to turn around and never look back seeing myself not scared anymore and hopefully I can tell her what I kept from her then I will know that this was all done for us to be here. Man, I was like a little kid in the living room trying to shake open my present that she wrapped for me a medium size box just didn't know what it was but was happy she did buy me something as I wrapped hers up in a small box that had Kim Butter even more excited than me. Going to bed that night and not waking up until that next day was Christmas and I woke up like a little kid wanting candy that I just kissed her that morning with us having the radio all night holiday music it was so great to go over there and unwrapping my gift. I saw that it was a nice sweater that I loved it with gloves and then she kissed me again saying Merry Christmas as I told her I love her then gave her gift she ripped it quick open it seeing a bracelet with her name signature written out then the watch too that all I got was kissing all over my face. She put it on and was wearing that thing good what a wonderful day. As we just hugged each other loving this day then as we had some breakfast of course watching on tv the parades as her parents called saying Merry Christmas and it was so nice that both of us got chance to talk with her niece and nephews too. She was on that phone talking while about what I gave her all happy so I was just smiling from ear to ear glad that nothing going to take what we have away even though my parents will be calling soon too with us only have one line not two way I think. By time she finished talking to everybody it was going on 12pm knowing it just a matter of time before my family be calling so need to get ready. With her still happy then it came time to talk to my parents as they called 5mins later saying Merry Christmas to me and Kim Butter was nice as that dad got on phone too then I let them know we having an enjoyable time how Kevin and Bernadette then Kim Butter told them she has gift for them and will be seeing her parents but won't see you which was okay. As I told them I will see them today and hope yall okay haven't heard from Jevone will he be there and mom said she didn't know but can you still come so I said yes as she asked did we buy them something I just said we didn't have enough money tight for the wedding as I said I see yall later. But before I hung up and the strangest thing was said to me that dad saying he loves me and I the only son that respect him and he miss me like I just saw yall month ago but I had to ignore that like it's all about fact he can't touch me and I be with my future wife now so he must love mom. As time was going by Kim Butter wanted to hurry up and go see her family then I chill over there and then head to my parent's comeback pick her up so that was the plan as I wore that beautiful sweater she bought me as she wore her gift. Got over see her family with their little tree in the living room nice and all her family over good to see them welcome me with a big Merry Christmas smile that I not use to at this time of the year so I couldn't leave rite away. As we chilled her family gave me some sox and gloves were nice get gift not even from my family then watched tv with her dad and brother we played with the video games of football on tv was nice to see and it was a fun time nobody mad just joy. By time I had played 3 games then it was time for me head over to my family as I kiss Kim Butter saying I be back then I asked could I call my family on their phone her mom said yes so, I called mom picked up phone I told her I at her family house getting ready to leave like I still live with them. Then her that father said he wanted to say Merry Christmas to them so I gave him phone they spoke and her mom too just hoping my parents don't say anything silly but didn't. Then I just said okay got to go bye and all I knew was that was a front but for how long knowing her family is sweet that I glad to soon be a part of this family. As I headed out Kim Butter said don't let them get you upset hurry back so we can enjoy rest of our night as I understood then left out knowing I need to go over there with the weather cold and not any sign of snow but they did say it would so didn't want be there when it happens. Driving over there took 45mins with no traffic that when I got there it was after 2pm that dad open the door hugging me like I just came home from service then mom kiss me and I hugged Kevin and Bernadette as Jevone and his wife was there too it was glad to see them. We all just chilled in house watching tv as that dad ask how Kim Butter family was, I said great they bought me sox and gloves as mom just stared saying okay nice but we didn't think buy you anything and that was it but all I wanted to do was see Kevin show my face eat then go back home. When you stay too long they start knit picking on your business don't have time for that as Jevone and his wife were quiet like they had something on their mind but hope it nothing as we there for a while watching tv as time flew by and the weather changed with little snow falling that was my exit to leave saying got to go pick Kim Butter up from family take her home. Mom was mad I leaving but that dad checked her saying that what man supposed to do jump for him wife laughing but I didn't think that was funny. Still, I said bye to everybody kiss Kevin as mom said why don't Kim Butter call us what she doesn't like us as I said no, she is busy working and help her family a lot but left it at that hugging Jevone and his wife as they left rite with me and I knew I left rite time got in car blowing my gone horn signal. I breathed regular after getting out there unscratched but sweating glad that dad didn't come over to me and say something upset me guess with Jevone around couldn't do it so it made it easier for me to just leave out because I know this is just the beginning of what's more to come with my parents knowing them they got a lot sneaky stuff do to break up not just me and my life but also Jevone too even though he already married. Just the fact my parents have nothing good I can learn from them take in me getting married so I know that I been learning from Kim Butter parents been together long time is the rite representation. Was therek up Kim Butter I started to feel better now seeing I did rite thing leaving because they still will not give up on leaving me and my brothers alone and let us lives. I made it back to her parent's house just talking to myself making sure I do not tell her the smart stuff they said keeping secrets from her not sure how much longer I can keep piling up inside this that one day it might be too much for me to hold in. As I got out car went to get Kim Butter her family house still happy kids playing with their toys and stuff it was better than being at my parent's place but she was tired and ready go home relaxed so I hugged everybody saying Merry Christmas as we left out but she asked me how was it I just said okay they still same but Jevone and his wife there they nice that was it as she knew I was lying but didn't want to let it mess up or time together as we got home and relaxed that holiday for us. As we continued enjoying it into the weekend still now that Sunday asked her what we are doing for New Year Eve and she said going out dancing it up to you as I did not care longs I with you going into new year. But still she was curious did my parents say anything smart about her family and I said no but she did not believe me knowing I lying just did not want talk about them as I was getting mad saying leave it alone okay then she just said fine because every time we are close to keeping peace my family finds a way to creep into our lives all over here. The week was short everybody at job glad to end this year on a good note I was just trying to get thru it without me and Kim Butter arguing about my family into the new year. But even with work busy deadlines of signs and discount prices needed to be made there was almost no time for lunch just taking break with my Supervisor Mrs. Tricia on us like a hawk making sure every sign application is done so me, Malandy and the Puerto Rican guy Alfonso back from his vacation there was no time for playing. Then I knew it would happen with my parents having our home# now they were calling our apartment like ridiculous asking why didn't I call them when I got home say if I had a fun time silly stuff like that. So, leaving messages like that on answering machine and Kim Butter getting home before me upset she listen then erase them before I got home still tell me about my parents and all I could do was say only tired of them then head to room try to sleep it off while she on phone calling her people letting it out. All that nonsense happening kept me from being in front of her that I hide in bedroom away from her so we don't get into wanting talk about my family what's wrong with them nonsense. As I kept my mouth shut even hearing her talking about them with her mom too thru those couple days seem like 2 weeks that by the time I knew it was New Year Eve. I finally had come out of my cave from either going bed early or waking up middle night to watch tv scared to fall asleep with me still off and on having those bad dreams of that dad chasing after me keeping that from her too. Then before going to work that last day in year I waking up I asked are we doing anything for New Year Eve going out as she just looked at me like I was saying I don't know then left without waiting on me for work and I knew then that was not a good sign so I need to make it before new year. Now I was in bad mood at work but couldn't show it to my coworkers they get suspicious like is the wedding off stuff like that as I kept working my job and that's all I did even going on break by myself talking to myself like that dad always messing with me sick of him and mom trying to mess up my happiness with people seeing me talking to myself in gallery I had to stop it as my eyes would get watery then heading back job clean my face. I was so quiet that just trying to finish the day ready leave out saying goodnight and Happy New Year to everybody still not talking much as Malandy and Alfonso ask me what I doing just said chilling in house with Kim Butter that's it we still saving for wedding that we toast in the apartment. Said later to Lanley and Sufon as I was out heading home but wanted to stop by flower store give her a rose say sorry for argument and love her hope this help as she was already there. When I got in she open door I had rose as she was better kissing me then we hugged and relaxed thru rest of the night watching tv and waiting for that night to celebrate 1994 closer to our future time together. As she had stopped off at the liquor store to get us something to drink I wasn't a drinker so she bought us 6pk coolers and we drank that up till it was time for countdown 5,4,3,2,1 Happy New Year 1994 we kissed and hugged then her family calling and of course mines too but it was our night and continued that into the New Year thank god he fixed it that what god put together nothing can separate our love for each other.

22

TO DO US NOT DEPART

Waking up so late in morning all them coolers in us she had most of them I just had two that was it for us that we stayed in bed for while trying to get it together cold with winter hearing curling up under each other in sheets. Then later got it together to watch some parades as we chilling then she checked all the messages and called her family as I didn't have any reason call mines don't want to be bothered last year mess this new year not having it but still stop talking about it and do something would be better. We had our love for each other back into the new year hugging and playing around as she finally got off the phone because Kim Butter can talk for hours with her people like I never seen woman do before. That was all about us weekend that we were calculating how much we owed on stuff and it was looking great that we had paid off more than 60% of our trip and reception I was so happy and shock but she was taking care of everything I just gave her the money that's it. The weather for new year was cold and some snow on the ground too so we go out there that Sunday and played in it that was that kid in us then go food shopping with car all happy but had to be careful driving in that mess and I was a good driver too. Hate to say I learn from that dad the one thing he did rite teaching me all I can remember him being a real dad beside the providing part too but rest is blackout as I was seeing this starting my life over with person love me not love and hurt me too. Time was over as reality kicked in back to work with us enjoying that peaceful Sunday night that it was so quiet I thought the phone was off hook no calls came in. Kim Butter doing that looking out for us not be bothered just hope there wasn't any family emergency as I let her know as she looked at me no you thinking about your family too much it's our time and I had to shut up after that. Then heading bed ready to start new work week moving closer to our marriage together as we slept good with the apartment nice and warm too that I wasn't scared to go sleep knowing the bad dreams of that dad chasing me but didn't have one and was so happy I jumped out bed ready to go back to work this new year. As we got going she was already dress and we drinking our tea together then left out catching trolley so happy that our heat for each other kept us warm thru the cold snow outside. Just sitting next to her on trolley my eyes was all on her and it was great that she almost missed her stop off Hightenstreet then I still had my 4 stops to eighty street but was missing her already. I got to work cloud nine and saw all my coworkers saying Happy New Year as everybody responded with gladness even to my Mrs. Tricia then seeing Malandy and Alfonso we talking about how great it is to have made it this year as they talked about their partying out while I said me and Kim Butter chilled and it was wonderful then running into Lanley and Sufon talking about they were with their wives that was nice to hear. I felt so much peace and love from my job that nobody was out to get me like we family and that is why I know who I need to be asking in my wedding because with Kim Butter talking about she wants 4 bridesmaid I need to have 4 groomsmen and I already have Jevone just need to ask Lanley and Sufon and Kim Butter brother Roney would be nice so I ask them this week give them heads up. That first week of January 1994 was so good that nothing could take my joy that this year was ours and finish going home to the best woman in my life my best friend that I never had. She opened the door with nothing but loving smile as I got in had some tea again because still cold outside sometimes having to walk up hill like 10 blocks because when miss the bus have to walk down 10 blocks to get another one then we catch trolley. As we chilled in apartment that following Saturday but still had to get downtown to pay on her dress, the reception and honeymoon trip too as she had me not waist time even the bad weather didn't stop what she wanted for us to have. Still taking care of our business then she would have us go to her parent's house and do some shopping for her family with her dad working times on the weekend making that money and that was her caring for her family that I loved about her. Times we did that it be hours that the day be almost over but then I didn't mind because going over there to play video sports games like football time with her brother Roney then her niece and nephews sometimes stop by too. Her parent's house was place to be at if you needed to not be mad anymore about something they come over there was spot. So, after doing that for her mom we headed home and it felt good doing for her family what they lack still didn't take their joy where they cussing or fighting like my parents did all the time. Things was going good for us for the next couple of weeks thru January and February but it started to happen with my family this a new year as they were calling us a lot asking where we having the wedding and do we have money for a reception plus honeymoon but wasn't offering us anything living in that expensive house in New Jersey. All I know is that I had to stop letting them leave those messages on answer machine always on weekends are you there I know your are there pickup like I am kid no respect was with Kim Butter looking at me and mad so I had to standup and protect her but still didn't want to make my parents mad. So I tried to talk real nice to them again as Kim Butter was hitting my arm saying stuff you too nice but she don't know how far they can threaten our wedding day by hurting me not showing up. I then had to tell her let me talk and then she went into bedroom as I talk my parents saying we fine but can yall help us out pay for some things and then mom was like no we can't that's when I just said fine but any money will help us. As I knew it was coming mom said why isn't her family helping her aren't they contributing and I just said yeah lying that's when Kim Butter heard little saying they not talking about my family as I tried to calm her down but then said okay love yall got to go and thanks hanging up. I knew Kim Butter was mad saying they got some nerve asking about my family when they ones living in that house like they better then stuck up. After she ranted for hour as I listen then she calmed down I just told her you know my family is okay I wasn't expecting them help us because they didn't help Jevone either and hugged her saying we still doing this okay as we went out to get some air that weekend as we both did not even caring how cold it was that day a change of atmosphere was necessary. By time we got back got something to eat came home still with of course my parents call back messages but just erased them getting ready for work week and focus on our wedding day that's it as she said I don't care who don't show up we still getting married and I heard that. With the month of February being Valentine Day coming soon I had plans to express how much I love Kim Butter but not buy anything too expensive because we tight like a dozen roses and to the movies too. Then things at job was changing as we were moving to the mailroom which is bigger more space and the mailroom was moving somewhere else but good for us have more space for our desk and the big color photo copying sign machine too. It was great for us that we not all tight in that old office plus close to the elevators to escape outside easier too as I was already looking at the drawings Mrs. Tricia showing us and I took my desk immediately with Malandy behind me and Alfonso was coming off like he tired of this job saying he won't be moving with us like okay. Just knowing he was leaving I was happy for him but still that mean more work on us and all new format signs we need somebody else to type them up too. So, of course they started looking for replacement until he was gone thru the month of February that it took a while into Valentines week that I was all about loving my baby and also Kim Butter had spoken to the pastor of the Presbyterian Church on Saymen Avenue about us getting married there and that we have to take class to get us ready for marriage at his church so I was nervous about that which was in

March so I had time. Love was in the air in the departments with so many women working in our offices that us guys were under pressure to step up our game for our ladies in our lives so I was making sure I did have the money to buy her those dozen roses and take her out to the movies. But the weather still cold out not that bad wasn't stopping us so that day before I was preparing but then had got a call at job from my parents that dad calling me saying hi son like he been a that father to me really. So, asking me did I send your mother a Valentine Day card for her and I said I will sorry just need yall address as he got mad saying that is your only mother and she loves all yall at least one of her kids can do that for her because she was talking all sad none of her kids love her. What a guilt trip put on me with us trying to do our wedding plans but I couldn't get upset in the office just played it off saying okay I got to go back to work then always something last saying I love you and she is taking you away from me that was nasty as I just said bye okay. That was so wrong say that to me at work that I was bothered by it messing me up thru that day knowing I still had to finish work then go home as I was quiet with my coworkers noticing change in me and I stayed that way even home to Kim Butter as she notice too but all I said I had a rough day just want to rest in bed so she let me. Still, she knows me asking did my parents call and Upset me I had to lie again saying no just a lot of work that's all okay and she left it alone that I went into that cave again only eating then sitting infront tv not wanting go bed again mode. All Kim Butter could do was just leave me alone I feel asleep in front of the tv that she had to come out room get me as next day was Valentine Day and I still had to take care of my baby going to work we walking I was feeling little better kissing her saying love you then we got trolley she went to work I to my job but had plans to surprise her at work on my lunch bring the roses up there she deserves it. Work was busy with Malandy helping me and Mrs. Tricia because Alfonso of course had taken time off not trying to be working here those last 3 weeks before we move and us still looking for at least a temp to help us but they think we are just fine so be it. As the day was going by and it was my lunch time and I had ask Malandy what her boyfriend was getting her for Valentine Day and she just said nothing probably he might cook for me something nice we stay at home as I said that is still nice of him then told her I going to Kim Butter job to surprise her with a dozen roses as she was so happy for me saying that is nice. Not letting my supervisor know that I left for lunch I waited for her to go to lunch then 10mins later went gallery get the roses and headed on the el train on my way. By time I got there it was 20mins went by but still had to go front desk ask for her while people were looking at me like okay then like 10mins later she had come off the elevator looking for me and I was hiding behind the roses just called her name she came at me smiling from ear to ear. All I know is I want to keep her happy before and after we get married and learn that not from my parents but her parents will to stay together not because of money but real love. I kissed her say Happy Valentine Day baby and she gave me a professional kiss then took the roses saying they beautiful and had to get back to work kissing me saying love you as I was leaving like yes I the man and went back to work that is my future wife. Got back to work only over like 8mins but Mrs. Tricia wasn't even back good thing Malandy ask me how it go I told her she was surprised and loved it she was happy for me and I know the rest of the love is on tonight. I was working my body off get out here on time as things worked out except one thing I had to call my mom but at job wish her happy Valentine Day get that out way. So, it was after 5pm and she is usually home by then as I called and she answered I said hey mom happy Valentine Day she said thanks then told her I sent you a card hope you like it as she asked did I get Kim Butter anything I said just taking her out but got to go love you and hung up didn't want to hear any negativity because felt it coming on. I was gone and by time got home she was there waiting for me saying she rather go out this weekend but wanted to thank me for the gift and that was the rest of my night. The next day I felt like superman all energized by our love and took that finish week strong all my signs then our weekend was still Valentines going to movies all about her and then still on cloud nine going to work that next week too with the roses lasting till that following Friday. Even the weather sun was coming out melting all the snow good to see but still with next week March we had that meeting with the pastor of the church we getting married to so we needed to talk about what they might ask us like why we want to get married and stuff like that hoping I don't make a fool of myself. Now with her dress almost paid off as we went downtown that weekend to make another payment then checked out the hall for our reception on dandler street in south Philly it was nice with a big basement all set up too and had parking. All I know is Kim Butter sure know how she wants her wedding to go and she making sure it's our one time great for us to celebrate and not discriminating who will help us either because you can't always depend on your race to come thru. All that running around had us tired and heading home full of happiness that Kim Butter was saying see things are working out and with our income tax we pay off the rest of the trip and reception hall too because when she puts her mind to something she does it. As we got home them phone messages were left because all I saw was like 8 messages and I know her family don't even call us like that so I knew who it was but had turned the volume down while I listen to them while she was in the bathroom and it was that dad saying Kevin not feeling well having two seizures that they might take him to hospital and this is your brother need to call us back make sure he okay. All those messages were about me calling back but then to what give me a guilt trip like are they doing this to my two other brothers too man but I hope Kevin is okay don't want nothing to happen to him I love him so I just told Kim Butter that Kevin had two seizures and called them to see he is okay. She just said don't fall for them using him to get at you okay but hope he is ok as she went into bedroom and I immediately called as mom answered saying what took you so long Kevin was in the hospital all that time but did you care no, but if that was her family you jump for her. I didn't want to argue just asking is he okay she said yeah but just because you getting married shouldn't forget about us then I said sorry and then told them keep me posted okay as they were watching him and all I know I was feeling bad worried about him as Kim Butter said is he okay I said for now they watching him she saw my face I was upset telling me he going to be ok they trying make you feel bad knowing she rite but that is my brother not hers. The next couple of days even as I went to work that week was calling the house checking up on Kevin and that dad said he is doing better I was happy but still messing with me saying he miss me I am his favorite son only one didn't fight him and love you as I started to get sick saying don't say that okay stop saying that stuff to me or I tell mom okay then I said bye. I was so mad he still saying that to me that I walked out the office to men's room hitting the doors knowing he keep saying that until I do something and I will watch me I tell mom on him because I still going to get married no matter what's going on. Man was I nervous even more that it was that Monday we see the pastor about marriage so that Monday was stay calm time and don't talk to my family as we went to work snow melting away while we were walking down hill because driving was costing us too much to park downtown and I started to get meter tickets too that I didn't want Kim Butter to find out about or she will beat me up. As work was still busy but they did bring in a temp to help us with work but she just copied our signs to color was better than nothing because I was trying to clean my mind for what pastor going to ask me. By time it was heading toward time go home Kim Butter called me from her job telling me am I ready for tonight I barely said yes then saying little nervous but she said we be fine love you so I then I had a thought to ask to of my groom men Lanley and Sufon being married what should I expect question ask of me. Before I left out went to them and Lanley with Sufon just told me ask about my relationship with god means to me and what it means to me to get married in eyes of the lord stuff like that so they did help a little just didn't give me the answer that comes from myself. By time I was heading home almost there was talking to myself trying answer two questions like I know god wakes me up he the reason we are breathing alive and the other is because God is the one that put every marriage together and we have to honor his ways of doing it. I know probably wrong but at least I trying while I wonder if Kim Butter have a better answer that I got to tell her what

I think so we can be on same page is what Lanley said to be for the pastor to see us as a couple as one in this marriage too. Our meeting was at 6pm so we had 30mins to get ready and all Kim Butter said to me say what's in your heart so I went with that as we took the car to get there being it's on Saymen Avenue got there on time. As we met the pastor and things went ok that he did ask us those two but others that after all being nervous it went great and still had one more meeting with him then saying he see we are meant to be married was good news but needed to see him that Wednesday so we let in good spirit. All I know is that things are getting better as we get closer to our wedding with Kim Butter telling me we pretty much paid her wedding dress and then almost the receptions plus the trip too will use our income tax so everything is going to her plans. As those two days went by fast it was that next meeting with the pastor and after it was over, he had approved us to be married in his church he would do so next stop marriage here we come. What a great way to head toward our weekend but still had to pay the church too and she had to let him know how many people so that was her department I just make the money. Now tired of him talking to me like a little boy I was so tired that I didn't want to be bothered by them for a while until I feel like it but will hope they okay but not jumping worrying every time they call because they mad can't have me to control anymore too bad. The next couple weeks I just tried to block thinking about them out not worrying about Kevin or Bernadette but on us getting married and thru the couple of months did exactly that with Kim Butter helping me keeping me busy running around downtown and stuff then also talking to my four groom men where to go to get their tuxedos and get hookup like a discount for them too. But still my parents pursued calling me leaving messages like Kevin okay but we not feeling well things like that so I can call or run over there but would wait until they sleep to leave message saying hope yall okay that's it because I didn't want talk to them or if I did, they would of had me. Even thru that month of April showers the weather was getting better outside as we heading toward May and making the payment to the church since filing our income taxes and getting a good amount back then went downtown a weekend paid off rest of trip and then other things. While Kim Butter was taking her bridesmaid to get the colors and their dresses fitted and made for them too so she was having me driving everywhere as her chauffer I was too for my baby so she can get us to it more when I become her husband. Even at work it was busy with all 10 stores asking more and more for those colorful with photos on them signs that we were getting overwhelmed and needed another coworker because Alfonso had left out gone but finally things change. It was sometime in May when we were introduced to a new coworker Fannie and she was nice I believe she worked somewhere else in building but was glad to meet her as she was tall woman nice and immediately Mrs. Tricia put her to work on typing but she had these long fingernails that I was wondering how she going to learn to type or did she ever do that. I didn't care how just as long as she help us out even if she just ran copy machine using one finger push the button use her because it was like me and Malandy was multiply task typing, printing then copying our own charts into color was . So now with that on my mind I still hadn't talk to my parents asking are they coming to my wedding and need to get into with Jevone to get him fitted at my tuxedo place wear the right colors too black and white. I had to do this not at home where Kim Butter gets upset thinking I begging to their will like really need them to be there but if it was up to her, she wouldn't care if it was just us getting married. So, going to the gallery I use the phone calling my parents knowing May is almost over but at least I giving them 4 months to still come to my wedding and will beg if I have to just want someone there if I had to ask or threaten that dad I will because all I done keeping this secret to protect the family while still hurting is not a lot to ask from him. The best time to make that phone call to my parents was the day at work and it was that day during middle week of May that I had to make this call even though still trying keep peace talk nice to them don't want that dad to forget what he still owe me. So, it was on my lunch and I went to a pay phone calling them with that dad at home watching Kevin as he said hi son like really but anyway, I just got to point saying so will you and mommy be coming to my wedding September 9th is the day as he was like why should we come you don't love us after all I done to protect you the guilt trip again. All I could do as I was getting upset just said please can yall come after all I done for you keeping this secret please convince mom and Bernadette to come to my wedding okay I still haven't told anybody so please because Jevone is my best man and his family is coming and Kim Butter is too. That's when he said okay I see but then saying he miss me because mom still don't love him stuff like that as I said okay love yall and mommy okay thanks then had to hang up as I was walking around about to cry a little with things he still said to me don't need to think about that stuff now. For the rest of the day I was just quiet didn't want to talk to anybody or my coworkers trying to do my job as the new coworker was talking and laughing with Malandy was good to see I didn't really talk to her that much though but she seem nice just little loud talker. Then still finish work heading home with all that junk in my head got in and Kim Butter there asking was I okay I just said yes tired did a lot of typing today ask how her job was she just said a lot going on processing claim she does then just want her to hold me like a mother holds her child make them feel better. She knows me that I was not telling her everything and would just leave me alone but comfort me was great loving things about her why I lucky man to be marrying this beautiful fiancée as we chilled thru that night. Later I still woke up middle night seeing that dad in my dreams and had to get up as I did wake Kim Butter up a little all I said I need to be left alone she was not happy with that still trying to figure out what kind of dreams am I having about my family but then couldn't keep arguing with me just let me be was best thing. Ended up sleeping on couch falling asleep then waking up the next day frustrated what I have to go thru to have my family come to a day that every relative would love to see a son getting married not a bad kid or disrespected his family cussing or having babies out there but doing it the way Jevone did it. Then reality kicked in and I knew it would be such a fight to asked them with that dad knowing I never hurt him like he done to me year after year then letting mom think I disrespecting them by leaving starting my life with my fiancée after I was the last one to leave defending them when Jevone and Terance left and always breaking up the fights the peacemaker but now where is my peace for me at still trying to find it. It just seemed like the closer we were getting to be married more drama came me like if I was not getting married and still living with them they be all up in my face happy I stuck with them but that is not the case. So hard with no one to open up to never having a best friend that my parents hide us like in a cave no fun or meeting new kids and now about to be with the woman of my future it's going to be hard for me to open up to her on such deep and scary things that happen to me don't want her to think she made a mistake. As I did what usually do don't say anything and kept it to myself then had to call Jevone and make sure he will be in my wedding as I talk to him asking him how is the married life, he just said its wonderful and her family is so nice to me that he knows he made rite decision while I was telling him mom and dad trying to hurt me now not come to my wedding either. Jevone said they never want us to be happy so you better not let them stop you from marrying either that he tried to tell me before he left that they will turn on you too and now I see he was rite all along. So, I just let him know the tuxedo store and the color too as we talk for a little that evening while Kim Butter was in room relaxing and then let him know it be four groom men okay then ask can you get in touch with Terance and ask him to come to please so he said okay telling him love you man hung up. See I not only one with problem with them that even his new relatives probably see it now too but his new wife still with him so that's a good sign she loves him a lot and I know mines loves me after stuff she seen and we not even married yet. All me and Kim Butter worked on was making sure we had everything covered from flower boy she wanted her nephew and niece walk down and then Nenya her sister is maid of honor. Then the limo company we be having pick us up another bill then making sure the reception place has our food the wedding cake there then while she was at the dress place, I said I will be back and went took her engagement ring to jewelry store on 8th chestnut had money from income tax to get us matching wedding rings because I told her I take care of the rings checking out couple stores after walking around down there found the rite store and matching rings. Told the jeweler I am getting married in September need these before so he gave me a great deal done my part getting back to her in time as we headed home so she could talk to her bridesmaid on their dresses. There was no time to enjoy our weekends together too busy out getting money from our people pay their outfits off picking up her bridesmaid get them fitted and my groom men too because in a blink of eye September will be here. And the thing was all I was doing was her chauffer all the time Kim Butter didn't know how to drive nobody taught her but we did what we had to do including sending out the invitation to everybody that wanted to go but of course one time she was getting nervous as 4mos went to 21/2 months left for us now that July is here. I didn't even care about my birthday since all our funds was to make sure everything is paid off for wedding not owe nobody nothing that I had to pay the limo driver too and the time we have it which Kim Butter said for at least that whole day. See with her mom and friends at her job that are married helped her do it rite was nice to know plus they were also going to give her a bridal shower at her job that I knew about as I was supposed to also have my last being single out with Lanley, Sufon planning it also Jevone and Roney there too. Even people at my job were happy for me mostly everybody on the 8th floor were glad for me knowing Kim Butter use to work there she still talk to some inviting them to her wedding too as I ask my coworkers too. It's been some tight past couple of months because we still had to pay our rent then with us taking this honeymoon trip to Sidney that we still needed money down there and nobody really helping us that every penny went to make this a rememberable wedding for my baby. So, my birthday July 23rd came and went that only gift I wanted was chill with Kim Butter no going out spending just balloons and card was all love I needed as she still was my rock in our relationship while I was the worrying not sure my parents are coming to my wedding. I knew I had to do something with it so close and I went to call them at work but this time not trying to hear no guilt trip as that dad answered said hi son and I said so are yall coming to my wedding because you owe me that dad with me not telling anybody you owe me. Next thing I hear him quiet then says okay we be there and I love you for being there for me ok sorry that happen okay you are my favorite son. Then it hit me and came out of nowhere started tearing up like a river all that heaviness of him hurting me not coming was off me as I was in the office at my desk trying to hide my face crying saying thanks and asking did mommy like the invitation he said yeah and that he loves me so I said love yall too got to go. That little boy inside of me was crying like as I had to go to men's room with it stuff still inside me just need to be that man and husband my future wife needs to see because I don't want to go back there all that pain and abuse when I seeing my happy life in front of me and still love my family just they need to love our decision to be happy and hope my parents get theirs back. All I wanted to do is now get ready these last two months before I become a husband to my future wife and not let my past mess up our future including my parents but happy her family be there from what I seen but don't know if she had any issue with hers so it's looking like everything is a go now all we have to do is just show up and I believe that god will do the rest. During that last couple of weeks we had plans to go pickup her wedding dress and stuff I couldn't look at or her see my tuxedo plus have the bridesmaids dress ready too so it was important to communicate to all of them so they don't cut us short with her wanting to have four bridesmaid and 4 groomsmen. I then had to talk to my guys two coworkers at job their tuxedo needed to be paid and picked up no later than August 1st and then also Jevone two and my soon to be brother-in-law Roney. Later as the weeks we didn't do much of nothing but running around afterwork still getting Kim Butter jewelry for her to wear for the wedding too like something borrowed and something blue from family then her shoes and other stuff. But we couldn't forget had to get a photographer to take our wedding pictures but when I had asked Kim Butter about that she looked at me like I was saying I been taken care of that okay you late real late and I just started laughing that is my baby. So, my part still had to get my tuxedo clothes together as well also taking her parents and family shopping for outfits as well in last week of July so everybody down to the ring boy and girl looking beautiful and that was all I did was drive everybody around going to north then south Philly all over because we had to make sure our people had their stuff except other got it themselves. When we were done that weekend, the only day we chilled was Sunday me and Kim Butter because nothing was really open to do anymore shopping so that was our time to talk see how many people coming and also to reception with this week be August month one month to go it was crunch time so sleeping was all we did. Then as we went to work that Monday, she didn't know they will be giving her a bridal shower that I can't wait to see how surprise she be and I come up there to get all the gifts for her in the car this time can't take all that on bus. Kim Butter was so surprised and happy that she got a lot of gifts and support too even people that didn't really like her so I was happy for my future wife and had to then later afterwork pick her up meeting her coworkers was nice too. I was just happy how close it was I about to get married just couldn't believe it but of course my parents had called me couple times at apartment with mom saying they will be there trying to be nice now knowing Kim Butter family and relatives are supporting our marriage now don't want to look like that cast out. Don't know how long that's going to last but hope they act rite and respectful to Kim Butter family because they can't talk much with them faking paying for a house can't afford anyway but so at work it was all about me am I ready nervous you sure temping me girls up at the job saying you not going thru this stuff like that I ignored. By time my week was thru I was so tired but a little worried as Kim Butter was trying to keep it together but I know she was just as nervous as I was so we both just kept trying to relax and get our rest from all running and running for the past months making sure everyone's in position. Talking to Jevone the following week about him getting his tuxedo and he asked me how mom and dad been treating you I just said sneaky and mean stuff talking they wasn't coming but then just last week that dad said they are but who cares we still getting married. He then said they didn't come to mines except dad and yall so I just said don't worry they might act a fool especially now they said Terance coming with his girlfriend but I haven't even talk to him have you and he said yes he just out there so still mad at them but I didn't want hear that. I told him got to get rest but thanks for being my best man and can't wait to be married like you did it not looking back love yall then hung up. Still having my younger brother to talk to meant a lot to me just if he only knew what I been hiding from him for years he probably would have changed his mind of wanting that dad there at his wedding. We were coming down toward the time for me to get ready and release all that wanting to live a single life out my system as each day I was going thru it that I never had happen to me before there were women saying hi to me and looking at me like never before I mean I okay but a slim light skin guy like why they seeing me now. All this time I been single nobody even gave me time of day except my baby like what is it because now I found my partner and best friend that all of the sudden, I look okay now to talk too this was weird like even women at job was speaking to me and I just was in shock but it's okay I been decided who I want to be with but still nice to know I got it going on. So, with that making my head big and stuff I paid it no mind still going to work at my job but except her girlfriends here were letting me have it saying if I break her heart they coming after me including Malandy too while the new coworker just laughed of course we would. Then my guy coworkers were testing me saying you need to get on that one knee be ready to get down as I was like okay whatever but it was great to see they supporting me like that as then time was moving fast with the weeks going by as the month of August was almost over with a week to go. That's when Kim Butter was talking to me when we at home saying she loves me and is so happy to be marrying me that your family not going to stop us because we are one and don't let them intimidate you okay they better not try to mess up our day okay so I took that as I need to step up be her man and not a little boy anymore the time is now to speak up. While we enjoyed those last couple of weeks together loving each other it was heading toward the end of August and we with now our wedding day two weeks away that the fellas at the job were planning something for me and Kim Butter girlfriends also planning a ladies' night out for her. I was at the apartment talking to Lanley and he was letting me know what and where we be going because I wasn't a planner like that or knew the spots to go being in a cave until meeting Kim Butter so I was up for almost anything except Kim Butter said all loud while I was on the phone, he is not a drinker that he will get mess up on can of bear just so you know and Lanley started laughing like . That is all I needed now her to embarrass me like that but I love that about her always full of surprise but still it was on as I ask her where she going to and you better not do anything I wouldn't do as she just laughed saying whatever. I was so excited because when that Friday came Kim Butter was supposed to be going out for a girl's night single for last time and it was my night that Saturday September 3rd so all I could do was hurry up home from work wondering again where she going and what she be wearing too don't want her looking too hot only for me. She opened the door and all I could do was stare like she was naked or something because man she was looking great with a skirt on and popping lip gloss that I wanted to go with her as she was laughing at me but then her girlfriends came around 8pm calling her saying they outside so I walked her out kissing her telling her I wait up for you but she said it be too late as she left. It was okay because I know we be one married couple next Saturday as I just went into apartment and watch tv rest of night having it all to myself but still wondering is she going to get her drink on like never before because she can handle her liquor and I found that out a lot. By time I fell asleep it was late like after 1;00 am and then the phone rung it was her calling me she downstairs bet she was too drunk to open the door but I ran down steps instead elevator and she was messed up drunk but laughing like with her girlfriends screaming out the window car she all yours. Just glad she had a last nice time that I had to take her up on elevator tore up but still look good so I got her in apartment and immediately put her in bedroom and she was out under cover in 5 minutes but that is my baby. Now with her still sleeping the that Saturday morning I was still little nervous what the guys had for me but cool with whatever as by time Kim Butter woke up it was in the afternoon and she looked she was hit by a Mack truck all woozy and sloppy saying what happen all I did was laugh at her how beautiful she still looked but didn't kiss her needed that mouthwash. I was glad for my baby enjoying herself and coming home safely too not doing something she shouldn't do but knowing her she not going to tell me even if I asked her so I was fixing her breakfast and some coffee to wake her up but all she did was lay in the bed thru rest of day. As I was talking where to meet the guys Jevone couldn't make it but said have fun while Roney said he can go with me that's when Kim Butter came back to me saying yeah watch him telling her brother I am glad he is going. She then was telling me just how she glad be around good girlfriends that they ate and drank but not all of it just enough make me feel better then with her recovering it was getting toward my time to roll out as I said I going to get dress with the guys picking me up and that Malandy boyfriend was hanging out with us too because I would talk to him from time to time when he call for her seem like a nice guy. Then got dress and was looking okay she just said yeah you better not forget I only woman that can touch you so don't forget that as I was laughing saying I love you and will be careful as she gave me this nice kiss saying there is more where that came from walking me out to front where guys were there waiting. We then went to pick up Malandy boyfriend Antwain and he was ready as ever then we on our way all I know I was nervous but kept it together just knowing this is last time I do this single. Went to first spot in west Philly was nice and they gave me a drink immediately that look like water but it was thick as I took one shot and that what started my roller coaster ride as they were laughing at me with music playing and Roney looking at me while they all getting their drink on but then they started giving me more and another one that after the third shot I was laughing. Then it hit me that I had to go to bathroom letting it out already and hit the door wall almost fell out that Antwain had to come get me out of the stall so then knew I was in for it then went back to the table and it seem like hours went by but they said lets go to the next spot.

I remember being put into car in back we heading somewhere else but Roney said he is good heading home as my journey continued. Later was in and out of it with just having some shots of drinks then got half my mind together and next thing I knew we was at a spot then I was dancing for a while hearing music and next thing back into the car, we were out again to another spot then I saw everything. It was girls after girls coming up at me dancing in some unusual outifts that Lanley and Sufon was cracking up at me how I was looking at them they giving me more drinks and Antwain all up in it with us so it was a night I couldn't remember much but just all that skin in my face in my face as I remembered Kim Butter saying don't touch or something like that. By time we were done I was done for that night all singled out as we were heading somewhere else but I was hanging just my face outside the window to where we came to stop and it was Antwains place that all I remember he taking me out the car then next thing I know I hit the floor and that was it for me that night. What a way to enjoy your last single night out with guys that like you and respect what you doing not out to hurt you like my family did making me see being in that cave all I missed. As I do not even remember how or what time I woke up but all I know it was later in day because that sun hit my face and malandy was fixing me something to eat and by time I got it together that's when Kim Butter came for me and had a ride to take me back home with my wrinkled up drunk clothes on looking like a wino. She was laughing at me so much knowing they got me good last night but I still walked a little straight as we said thanks to Malandy and Antwain taking care of me was great friends then it was home James for me I was not about to do nothing but sleep rest of that Sunday and did that. As we got home she took safe care of me with tea and some soup for my upset stomach not wanting me to throw up all over the place and our nice apartment giving me a bucket everywhere I needed it what a sweetheart woman. Somehow, I got it together to still go back to work that last week with Kim Butter help that when I got back Lanley and Sufon had been telling the guys how they got me good for my last singles night out before I got it all I saw was my coworkers laughing at me and it was cool with me. Malandy had been told by her boyfriend how I was too so she had her laugh on with my new coworker too Shanell is her name that it was on for the rest of the day and somehow it spread to the mail room and other departments too know I getting married this Saturday that I had to just laugh along with them. I was like a slow turtle that day and thru the week that my Wednesday I knew that I had 3 more day to be married so I then got it together with everybody now calling us saying they coming and directions to the church plus that Kim Butter parents was trying to be in the limo with us but change of plans it just be her and her bridesmaid. Things were coming to that time as all I did was asking god to please make everything go rite for our wedding and not have everyone know this is our day. Then my last two days at work and I had Friday off to get myself ready and with some people from my job coming I said bye to them because after the wedding we headed for a week in Disney honeymoon so just said thanks to everybody glad to see me getting married and stuff knowing when I come back, I be a married man. I said my goodbyes to my boss then Malandy saying I see you at my wedding and rolled out excited but nervous to know hope I don't mess up my words to say to her but was going downtown to get our matching wedding rings out while Kim Butter went to get her hair done good so she looked beautiful as my future wife. As I took care of that headed home it was later in evening just talking to myself saying I getting married and still in shock that its me that skinny kid being picked on and abused all my life now I have someone that wants to spend rest of her life with me that made me almost tear up again. Getting home Kim Butter had just got in herself open door said are you okay and ready all I did was wow your hair looks beautiful hug her saying yes I ready and we going to have a great wedding I promise you that everything will be fine so we spent our night loving each other for the next chapter of our new lives. Then woke up that day was here we was up on time as I was out the door and had my tuxedo and she was up getting it together and I was out the door by 8:30 am waiting for my ride to pick me up but making sure her limo comes to get her she said he coming then kissed her before I left as my ride showed up but it wasn't Jevone still glad I had one as we headed to the church as I was cool just talking to myself. There I spoke to the pastor as he said are you ready and I just said yes but is my best man here because he didn't pick me up and that's when I saw Jevone say sorry couldn't get you but glad you made it then he helped me get dress but I was so nervous that I almost didn't have my socks until he told me calm down breath you be fine okay. I was so thankful Jevone help me and he was here as I was ready and started to look out the church with people coming in that I saw Kim Butter family and was little happy but didn't' see mines as Jevone said don't worry about that you still going to get married. As time was going by with our wedding supposed to start at 11:00 am it was already after 10:00 am and that bothered me but then he had me sit down then the rest of my groomsman showed up Roney, Lanley and Sufon all in their black tuxedo looking nice made me feel better. By that time, the pastor came in saying we are about to start and I was like okay nervous that Jevone said again breath and do you have the rings that's when I panic saying where they at that I was sweating like for 10:00 mins looking for them but finally found them giving to Jevone to hold. He was laughing at me but said you can do this okay and then it began as all I heard was the music playing and Jevone walked me out there as I was hoping still my parents showed that I didn't even look out there until standing at the middle of the church then seeing all these people and was like it's really happening. Then the music started and all sudden my heart was beating like hundred miles a minute and all I saw was this beautiful woman in white dress at the top church and her that father with her as she came closer and closer with the music playing that all I could do was stare at her like this is my wife and I am so lucky to be her husband. All I know is when her that father let her go to be with me in matrimony then standing infront of me as the pastor asked me those words do you take this woman to be your lawful wedded wife to love honor and cherish for sickness and health to death do yall part and I almost got stuck but then said I do. Then he asked her the question and the last thing I heard was till death do yall part she said I do and the pastor said may I pronounce you husband and wife as I kissed wife Kim Butter Cylence passionately. Seeing my life has changed forever of that Chapter of a New Pain Free Life is about to happen with the Wife and Love Of My Life that what was Hidden, God Has KingMe!! To Marrying My Queen, God Is Good!!

Printed in the United States
by Baker & Taylor Publisher Services